The Miner's Angel

EMMA HARDWICK

ROMANCE PUBLISHING

COPYRIGHT

Title: The Miner's Angel

First published in 2024

Copyright © 2024

Print ISBN: 9798342652445

Version: TMA-00001-P

The right of Emma Hardwick, identified as the author of this work, has been asserted in accordance with the Copyright Designs and Patents Act 1988.

All rights reserved. No part of this work may be reproduced in any material form (including photocopying or storing by any electronic means, and whether or not transiently or incidentally to some other use of this publication) without written permission of the copyright holder except in accordance with the provisions of the Copyright, Designs, and Patents Act 1988.

Applications for the copyright holder's written permission to reproduce any part of this publication should be addressed to the publishers.

The characters in this book are fictional. Any resemblance to persons living or dead is coincidental.

CONTENTS

Chapter 1	5
Chapter 2	8
Chapter 3	15
Chapter 4	19
Chapter 5	28
Chapter 6	35
Chapter 7	44
Chapter 8	48
Chapter 9	55
Chapter 10	58
Chapter 11	67
Chapter 12	72
Chapter 13	84
Chapter 14	92
Chapter 15	96
Chapter 16	100
Chapter 17	107
Chapter 18	111
Chapter 19	118
Chapter 20	129
Chapter 21	135
Chapter 22	142
Chapter 23	144
Chapter 24	154

Chapter 25	159
Chapter 26	168
Chapter 27	177
Chapter 28	185
Chapter 29	193
Chapter 30	198
Chapter 31	205
Chapter 32	211
Chapter 33	215
Chapter 34	220
Chapter 35	229
Chapter 36	234
Chapter 37	246
Chapter 38	254
Chapter 39	260
Chapter 40	263
Chapter 41	271
Epilogue	274

CHAPTER 1

1890s Wales

As the carriage rattled over the uneven cobblestone roads, Dr Ebba Chadwick peered out of the window at her new home. On that early Sunday morning, Cwmgryf, a Welsh mining village nestled in a valley surrounded by imposing hills, appeared rugged and unpretentious. Soot-covered cottages lined the streets as their inhabitants cast wary glances at the newcomers. The distant, constant hum of mining activity served as a reminder of the hardship faced by the villagers.

> "Here we are," Elliot murmured, his strong hand giving Ebba's a reassuring squeeze. "Our new beginning."

The carriage stopped outside a modest stone cottage, its walls damp with coal-tainted moisture. As the couple stepped down from the carriage, they were met with curious eyes and guarded expressions from the locals who had paused in their daily tasks to observe them. Newcomers were rare in this tight-knit community.

> "Let's start unpacking," Elliot suggested, trying to sound cheerful.

Together, they heaved their wooden boxes onto the cobbled path leading to their front door.

Inside the cottage, the air was heavy with the scent of damp walls and coal. As they carried box after box into the small parlour, Ebba couldn't help but feel a pang of nostalgia for the familiar surroundings of London. She shook off the feeling, reminding herself of the importance of their mission here in Cwmgryf.

> "Elliot—," she began, "do you think we'll be able to win their trust?"

> "Of course, my love," he replied, pausing to wipe the sweat from his brow. "It won't be easy, but we're prepared for that. We just need to show them that we're here to help, not to judge or change them."

Ebba nodded, bolstered by his unwavering confidence. Thanks to their shared upbringing, they both united in a steely determination to advocate for better working conditions and healthcare for the miners and their families.

> "Besides," Elliot continued with a wry smile playing on his lips, "you've never been one to back down from a challenge."

> "Neither have you," Ebba retorted with a grin, her heart swelling with pride for her husband.

Despite the weight of their responsibilities, they could still find moments of levity. Ebba's thoughts drifted to the villagers outside. She knew their curious looks held more than mere suspicion. There was an undercurrent of desperation in their eyes.

"Once we finish settling in we should make a point to meet as many of them as possible. Show them we are here to stay."

"That sounds like a plan, my dear,' Elliot agreed, his voice brimming with hope and determination.

And with that, they continued to transform their modest cottage into a welcoming home, ready to face the challenges that awaited them in Cwmgryf.

CHAPTER 2

The village fete in Cwmgryf unfolded under a vast expanse of blue sky, as dark clouds loomed ominously in the distance. Cheerful bunting fluttered in the breeze, adding some brightness to the scene. The air was filled with the aroma of freshly baked bread and the earthy scent of coal that seemed to permeate every aspect of life here. The newlyweds strolled arm-in-arm among the villagers, taking in the chaotic blend of laughter, music, and the raucous shouts of children at play.

> "Remember," Elliot whispered, giving Ebba's hand a reassuring squeeze, "we're here to meet the locals and show them we care. Let's start up a few conversations."

Ebba took a deep breath, her heart pounding in her chest as she looked around at the faces gathered at the fete. The expressions on the villagers' faces were a confusing mix of hope, scepticism, and even open hostility from some of the miners. She could feel their eyes on her and Elliot, sizing them up, trying to discern their intentions.

> "Of course," Ebba murmured, forcing a smile onto her face as they approached a group of women selling pretty handmade crafts.

They exchanged polite words, but the conversation felt tense, with the women's forced smiles hinting at a lack of trust. The villagers who worked in the mines often thought that professional people like the Chadwicks never bothered to interact with them, unless they had some ulterior motive.

As they weaved through the crowds, the couple felt the weight of their mission pressing down on them. It seemed like an impossible task to gain the trust of these villagers. Ebba turned to Elliot, seeking solace in his kind eyes. He returned her gaze with a tender smile and a gentle squeeze of her hand. But before long, the tenderness faded and Ebba's mind was filled once again with strategies and plans to bridge the gap between them and the villagers.

The sound of a warm voice floated towards them. Turning, they were met with the sight of a tall, lean woman with pretty features. She approached with purpose, her steps strong and confident.

"I'm Gwen Price," she said, extending a hand with a firm grip that belied her gentle nature. "The local midwife. I heard you'd arrived and wanted to welcome you."

Ebba took her hand, noting the roughness from years of hard work.

"Dr Ebba Chadwick," she replied. "It's lovely to meet you, Mrs? Miss?"

"Just Gwen," the woman assured with a warm smile, revealing deep dimples on either side of her mouth.

"Dr Elliot Chadwick," the Londoner chimed in, offering his own handshake.

"So, you're the doctor couple we've heard about," Gwen smiled before gesturing to the tall, sturdy tattooed seaman beside her. "This is my fiancé, Llewellyn."

"Nice to meet you both," Llewellyn said, his tenor voice deep and resonant.

Relief flooded through the newcomers at this unexpectedly warm reception.

"And as well as friends, we'll be colleagues. Did they tell you? The trust wants me to work alongside you. Heaven knows medical care is thin on the ground here. Please, let me introduce you to some of the villagers," Gwen offered, her enthusiasm contagious. "I'm sure they'll be more receptive once they get to know you. It's not you, of course. It's just they're not used to change, that's all. And perhaps that no one fights for these people's welfare. Ever. Well except the reverend."

"I can assure you that we will do everything within our power to protect them," Elliot confessed. "My parents have devoted their lives to running a Salvation Army citadel in London, that's actually how we first met. They graciously took Ebba in as a homeless child and secured her a scholarship."

"So, you two are childhood sweethearts. How lovely" Gwen cooed.

Ebba shared a knowing look with her husband and ally, feeling uplifted by this unexpected support. With the backing of Gwen and Llewellyn, navigating the complex web of relationships and politics within Cwmgryf might not be as daunting as she originally thought.

"We truly appreciate your help, Gwen," said Ebba as the couple followed Gwen and Llewellyn further into the fete, feeling a flicker of hope that they could earn the trust of these proud, hardworking villagers and make a positive impact in their lives.

Together with Gwen, Cwmgryf could become more than just a workplace—it could be a true home.

Amidst doubting stares from the locals, Gwen's enthusiasm for collaborating with the Chadwicks shone like a ray of sunshine through the dark clouds over the festive bunting and bustling stalls. The midwife's eyes sparkled with excitement as she spoke, her words brimming with eager anticipation. The conversation continued as they strolled along.

"I've heard a lot about your work, Elliot and I'm excited to learn from you. Your pulmonary training is fascinating to me. I'd love to do more than just deliver the babies'." Gwen said eagerly, her voice revealing her passion for her job.

"And you will, Gwen! We can start your training next Monday if you're ready?" Ebba chimed in, smiling as her new friend almost jumped for joy, touched by her sincerity.

Gwen whispered stories of the people they passed—their hardships, joys, and resilience in the face of adversity. Each tale painted a tapestry of life in Cwmgryf, a vivid picture that drew Ebba in and sparked her curiosity to know these people better.

"You must think I'm such a gossip!" Gwen exclaimed, blushing.

"Not at all. Thank you, Gwen," Ebba said, feeling more connected to the community with every story she heard. "Your insights are invaluable."

It was during one of these tales that a harsh voice cut through the sounds of laughter and music, causing them all to pause. The man who spoke was built like a barrel, his muscular arms crossed over his chest as he glared at Ebba and Elliot. Bryn Jones, an ogre with an abrasive nature and permanent scowl, eyed them with open hostility before striding over and confronting them. As he cracked his knuckles with a menacing expression, Ebba noticed two scarred and stubby stumps where a couple of fingers should have been.

"Who do you think you are, barging in here and trying to change our ways?" he barked, his tone dripping with disdain. "We don't need your fancy medicine. Our wise women's cures have served us well enough! You posh folks are always looking out for yourselves, making a pretty penny off of us with your sugar pills."

"This is Bryn Jones," said Llewelyn flatly.

Elliot bristled, his protective instincts on high alert, but before he could react, Ebba placed a calming hand on his arm. She knew that gaining the trust of hostile people like Bryn was vital, and reacting with anger would only fuel more distrust.

"Mr Jones, "Ebba said, calm and firm, "we understand your concerns and hold great respect for the customs and heritage of this village. Our goal is to work alongside you and share our knowledge and expertise where it can be of help. The Salvation Army has made a significant impact throughout the land, and with the local miner's trust, we want to extend that helping hand to South Wales."

Gwen was irritated by Bryn's rudeness.

"Bryn, you're aware that the benevolent societies provide crucial support for miners and their families," Gwen explained calmly. "They do more than just fund funerals and pensions. They work tirelessly to improve lives and prevent tragedies, as exemplified in Tredegar. The Chadwicks are committed to bringing that same level of care to Cwmgryf. You should appreciate that."

Bryn was taken aback by Gwen's words, which also sparked a silent understanding between the Chadwicks. They realised that earning the villagers' trust wasn't just about offering help; it was about demonstrating an unwavering commitment to their well-being. This was a chance to make a real difference, not just for Bryn, but for every soul in Cwmgryf who had been neglected for far too long.

CHAPTER 3

The evening sun was warm and golden as Ebba and Elliot Chadwick returned hand-in-hand to their humble cottage, contemplating the uncertain road ahead. Although the scent of damp walls and coal still dominated, they were determined to make this new place feel like home.

"Today was quite eventful, wasn't it?" Ebba mused as they entered. "Between Gwen's enthusiasm and Bryn's hostility, I'm not sure what to expect from this village."

"Indeed," Elliot agreed, taking off his hat and running a hand through his hair. "But we'll manage. We've faced plenty of challenges back in London, and we coped."

They unpacked their treasured belongings from the remaining boxes.

"We both know my specialist training in pulmonary care will be incredibly useful here. The miners are exposed to so much dust and fumes and suffer greatly from a host of respiratory problems. If I can prove that I can help ease their suffering with the latest methods, then there's our golden chance."

As they unpacked, the space began to feel like a real home. Their precious medical books found their place on the wonky shelves in an alcove. A small collection of framed photographs captured memories from their past lives together. Their wedding photo had pride of place, as well as a photo of the London Salvation Army building still run by Elliot's parents, John and Jess. A sense of hope and purpose settled into the room as they looked around.

> "Let's start with a free consultation day," suggested Ebba. "We can invite everyone in the village to come and talk to us about their health. That way, they can come to us and we can promptly address any simple issues before their very eyes. It's bound to start building trust instantly."
>
> "That's a brilliant idea," Elliot exclaimed, his eyes lighting up.

As they unpacked and talked late into the night, Ebba felt a mix of excitement and fear for the challenges ahead. But she knew that with Elliot by her side, they could make a difference in this remote Welsh village.

*

The disappearing sun painted long shadows over the small cottage that Ebba and Elliot Chadwick called home. Inside, a cool breeze swept through, causing candles to dance and making Ebba shiver as she cooked their evening meal.

"Elliot, can you check the window? The wind's getting in," she asked, her breath visible in the chill.

"Aye, I'll take a look" he answered, heading towards the twisted frame.

As he inspected it, he ran his fingers along the neglected wood, feeling the dampness that had seeped into its grain. As Elliot battled with the stubborn window, Ebba watched him with admiration for his persistence. But alas, the frame refused to budge, despite all his efforts.

"Looks like the frame's warped from the moisture. I'll try to sort it out tomorrow."

"Never mind, love," Ebba said, placing a comforting hand on his shoulder. "Come and eat."

Just as they sat down to relish a tasty bowl of piping hot stew, a knock on the door interrupted them: the arrival of a telegram for Elliot. With a mix of curiosity and trepidation, he carefully unfolded the paper. As he read the message, his expression grew pensive.

"Is everything alright?" Ebba asked, her husband's worried expression sparking her curiosity.

"It's fine. Just a note from the colliery," he said, quickly tucking the note into his pocket. "For now, let's just enjoy this delicious meal, before it gets cold, and each other's company. We've got plenty of time to talk about work tomorrow."

As they ate, Ebba couldn't help but think about the mysterious telegram. She found herself imagining different scenarios, each more worrying than the last, until she forced herself to stop. *'Stop being so silly. If it was important, Elliot wouldn't look so at ease.'* Tonight was a chance to settle in, find comfort in one another's presence.

As night fell upon Cwmgryf, Ebba and Elliot Chadwick lay in bed in each other's arms, their hearts entwined with the dreams and aspirations they held for themselves and the community they had selflessly come to serve. In the quiet darkness, they found solace and strength in one another, ready to explore the valley and greet its many inhabitants in the morn.

CHAPTER 4

Eager to settle both professionally and personally, Ebba Chadwick stood in her new yet modest clinic. The Trust had provided well for them, though there was still more that was needed. As the morning sun streamed through the window, casting a warm glow on the worn floorboards, she worked relentlessly, the shelves filling with medical supplies and simple equipment for their fledgling practice. She took a deep breath, inhaling the familiar scent of antiseptic —and the constant faint tang of coal dust that clung to the air in Cwmgryf.

Ebba busied herself with organising how to tend to her patients, despite being unsure of how many she would actually see. As a newly certified doctor, each day brought unpredictable challenges. She took care to neatly arrange bottles of iodine and store rolls of bandages, finding solace in the familiarity of her routine and boosting her confidence.

The clinic door creaked open, revealing a woman with a worried expression. She guided her adult son inside, supporting his weight as he shuffled alongside with a lolling head. His right hand was clutched against his chest, wrapped in a blood-soaked cloth. As he looked up to take in his surroundings, pain and fear flickered across his young face, his eyes wide and desperate.

"Dr Chadwick? I'm Mrs Evans, Mary" the woman gasped, her voice trembling. "Please, you must help my Henry."

"Of course," Ebba replied, her tone calm and reassuring as she approached. "Let me see his hand."

As Ebba carefully unwrapped the cloth, she assessed the injury's severity. Henry's fingers were crushed and mangled, likely caught in one of the mine's massive machines. Her heart clenched at the sight, but her expression remained steady, giving no hint of her concern.

"Can you tell me what happened?" she asked, her voice gentle as she probed for an explanation.

Using surgical tweezers, she carefully inspected Henry's hand with a precision honed through years of practice. Henry winced as he spoke, his voice strained with pain.

"Someone shouted my name when I was working the coal conveyor. I turned to look and my hand got caught between the belt and a pulley. It all happened so fast."

"Ah, I see."

Ebba nodded as her mind raced to determine the best course of action. She looked at the mother and, seeing the terror in her expression, decided to briefly distract the woman to help calm her.

"Mary, please fetch that bowl of clean water and some towels from the cupboard over there. We need to clean the wound properly before we can proceed."

As Mary hurried to obey, Ebba allowed herself a moment to collect her thoughts. The injury was severe. Henry might lose his hand if not treated swiftly and correctly. Yet, she could not allow her concern to affect her demeanour. She needed to exude confidence and assurance for Henry and his mother as she investigated one of the cuts that clearly went down to the bone.

"Dr Chadwick," Henry whispered, struggling to move his fingers. "Will I still be able to work?"

Ebba paused, feeling heavy-hearted at the uncertain future before them.

"I'll do everything I can, Henry. I promise."

The young doctor quickly gathered supplies and treated Henry's wound carefully, trying to ignore the tense atmosphere. As she worked, she couldn't help but wonder how many other young miners had been crippled by the dangers of their industry—and if her limited stockpile would last the month.

"Henry. You need to tell the colliery. The inspectors need to stop these accidents."

Mary looked despondent as she spoke.

"This was supposed to be a fresh start for us, Dr Chadwick. With my Dai sick and unable to work, we've been struggling to make ends meet. I thought if Henry could bring in extra income, we'd get back on our feet. And now this! Cwmgryf Colliery doesn't care. If the men can't work, you're out of your home and out of the village. The ogre who runs it, Charles Huntingdon, hates anything that cuts into his profits, and he despises complainers."

Ebba listened intently, her heart aching for the family's plight. already, she knew all too well the burdens that weighed heavily on the shoulders of mining families like the Evans.

"The Trust will do everything possible to help Henry, Mary. I promise."

With a plan of action forming in her mind, Ebba turned her attention back to Henry's hand.

"Good news is it doesn't look like anything's broken, young man. But I am going to apply some antiseptic and stitch up the deepest cuts. It won't be pleasant, but necessary if we want to save as much function as possible. Keep these bandages clean and dry, and come to see me if they need changing."

"I understand," Henry said, nodding, then clenched his jaw with determination as the stinging salve was slathered on.

Watching Ebba work with such skill and determination, Mary felt a glimmer of hope ignite within. This woman must have faced countless obstacles to train as a clinician, and now she was using her unwavering determination to aid the people of Cwmgryf.

"Dr Chadwick?" Mary hesitantly asked, "I know it's presumptuous but I'd be so grateful if you could look at my Dai too. He's been getting weaker by the day and I don't know what else to do. He wheezes all the time and, on damp days, he struggles for every breath. He's still struggling to make it to work when he can, but I don't know how much longer—"

"Of course, Mary," Ebba answered in a gentle and reassuring tone. "How about he comes on Sunday after chapel?"

As she bandaged Henry's hand, Ebba felt a renewed sense of purpose in her work. The challenges faced by the miners and their families were immense but they persevered, drawing strength from one another in the face of adversity.

As the afternoon slowly faded into early evening, the dimly lit consultation room grew darker, casting long shadows across the walls. A loud knock at the front door broke Ebba and Gwen out of their reverie. They quickly made their way through the short entrance hall, their footsteps echoing on the wooden floorboards. Gwen saw that the woman at the door was clearly in labour.

"Quick," said Gwen. "Lay her down there."

Soon, Bronwyn, the miner's wife, lay on the makeshift treatment table with sweat beading on her forehead. Her breaths were coming in ragged gasps and the air was thick with apprehension. The two women moved confidently around the room, preparing for the birth.

"Thank you for bringing her here. You can wait outside now, James," Gwen advised the man who was pacing around, wringing his hands.

"Alright, Bronwyn," Gwen said as she closed the door on him, her voice soothing and steady. "You're doing splendidly. Just remember to breathe through the pain."

Never having delivered a baby before, Ebba was grateful for the midwife's years of experience to draw upon. Feeling unsure, the doctor took Bronwyn's hand and gave it a reassuring squeeze, a fleeting memory of Elliot and herself discussing their hopes and dreams of parenthood flashed through Ebba's mind.

She could feel the woman's grip tighten as another contraction swept through her, pain evident in her eyes.

"Lean on us, Bronwyn," Ebba encouraged, her voice betraying none of her own concerns. "You're not alone in this. Gwen has delivered hundreds of bairns, just like yours."

The main area of the clinic was spacious, in stark contrast to the small consultation room that was attached to it. The examination table took up most of the space, and the lighting was dim with only one oil lamp providing a feeble glow. The equipment available for use was limited, but both Ebba and Gwen were already skilled at improvising with what they had on hand.

The women knew that every birth was still a precarious balance between life and death, and they were there to make sure Bronwyn and the baby's fate swung the right way.

"Gwen, I'm scared," Bronwyn whispered through gritted teeth, her eyes pleading for reassurance.

"Trust yourself and trust your body, Bronwyn," Gwen replied gently, her eyes never leaving the woman's face. "We're here to guide you, and together we'll bring your little one into the world safely."

As the hours passed, tension mounted in the room. Each minute dragged on slowly, marked only by the father's clicking heels and occasional requests for updates.

Despite the difficult circumstances, Gwen remained focused as she skilfully guided the baby's arrival.

"Keep pushing, Bronwyn," Gwen urged with determination. "You're almost there."

"Well done, Bronwyn," Ebba murmured, her heart pounding as the baby's head emerged. "Just a little bit more."

With one last surge of strength, Bronwyn delivered a healthy, slithering baby into the world.

The room itself seemed to collectively exhale as relief flooded in.

Gwen skilfully cut the cord, wrapped the baby in a clean blanket, and wiped its little cherubic face before handing it to its mother. Their eyes met in a moment of shared triumph.

"Congratulations, Bronwyn. You have a bonny little boy who looks just like his father," the midwife said softly. "You did wonderfully. I'll tell your husband to come in."

Ebba felt a wave of satisfaction wash over her as she sat jotting down Mary's case notes. While the day had been relentless, it was also a promising sign. She carefully added a final flourish to her eighth entry of the day, closing the ledger with a resolute snap. It seemed Glynlas was more ready for change than she had anticipated and the Trust would surely be pleased with this news.

Ebba was lost in a daydream when a soft knock at the door brought her back to reality. Gwen peeked into the room, holding a beautifully wrapped present. Ebba eagerly untied the ribbon and carefully unwrapped the cloth, revealing a mouthwatering batch of Welsh cakes inside.

"I found them on the doorstep! Somebody must be very grateful for you being here, Ebba."

"I wonder who sent them? Was there a note?"

"Sadly not. Anyway, I'll leave you to finish your records—then promise me you'll get yourself home!"

Ebba indulged in each delicious bite of cake, relishing the tranquillity after a hectic day. Her thoughts drifted to Elliot's first day at work and she couldn't help but wonder how it went. All she knew was that he had received a telegram summoning him to an early meeting at Cwmgryf Colliery at nine o'clock; they didn't even have a chance to talk before he left. She pondered if his day had been as demanding as hers.

CHAPTER 5

In the stuffy oak-panelled boardroom, Elliot Chadwick sat stiffly alongside other high-ranking mine officials and union representatives. Tension filled the air, a thick fog of unease hanging over them all. Sunlight struggled to stream through the window at the far end, partially blocked by heavy drapes. Sinister shadows cast across their grim expressions as each person braced themselves for heated and potentially explosive discussions ahead. With every passing moment, it felt like the walls were closing in on them, suffocating them with the weight of their collective responsibility and the insurmountable divide between their opposing stances.

"Mr Huntingdon," Owen Davies, the most senior union official began in a measured but firm tone, "I am sure you are aware of the latest inspector's report and the track record of the colliery, with its woeful safety record over the past year. It appears that whilst you have funds available to increase production, you are not investing in measures to protect your workers. These growing safety concerns must be addressed. I cannot sit idly by while conditions in the mine continue to deteriorate for our members, especially as you live like a lord when you visit London."

"Mr Davies," Huntingdon replied, his fingers softly drumming on the table, "I understand your concern, but the union must also consider the financial implications of implementing new safety measures. Profits are already strained and we cannot afford any additional expenses. As you are well aware, all of the inspector's recent recommendations have been implemented."

The union man clenched his jaw, feeling the frustration ripple through him like a tremor. He knew all too well that profits were the colliery owner's main priority and the current mine laws were still too lax to offer decent protection. Men like Huntingdon coast along doing the bare minimum—with the blessing of the government.

However, he couldn't understand how the man could be so callously indifferent to the lives of the men who worked tirelessly to line his pockets. The constant stream of desperate replacements willing to step into a dead man's shoes to work the seam meant there was little need for empathy from a colliery owner.

Observing the room, Elliot noticed a similar concern reflected on the faces of union representatives. They nodded in unspoken unity with Owen's words. Even one of Huntingdon's advisors gave a subtle nod of agreement from the corner of Elliot's eye. Feeling a fire of frustration growing within him and envisioning his crusading wife, the young doctor felt compelled to speak up.

"Sir," Elliot persisted, his voice wavering despite his efforts to steady it, "I speak to you as the head of the local Miner's Welfare Trust. I have seen the harrowing consequences of neglecting mine safety during my training. The latest public health study published in The Lancet on chronic respiratory diseases in Britain is shocking—over 200,000 men are currently gasping for breath every minute of every day, stricken by the relentless scourge of miner's consumption. Not only that, but fit and robust young men are being maimed or killed due to institutional failures. Surely you can understand the importance of safeguarding your experienced workforce. While mechanisation is increasing coal production, it still heavily relies on backbreaking manual labour."

"Dr Chadwick," Huntingdon said, leaning back in his chair with a patronising sigh, "I appreciate your passion and detailed understanding of the facts of this issue, but I must remind you that I have a business to sustain. The mine's continued operation depends on profitability. Without profits, the mine cannot function. If the mine shuts down, there will be no wages, leading to widespread unemployment in Cwmgryf. What good is having the safest mine if it goes bankrupt and is liquidated by the official receiver to cover its debts? Who would look at the books and choose to take over an unprofitable mine with so many others to choose from in the country? I must balance safety with economic viability to ensure the community's future."

The atmosphere in the room grew even more stifling, thick with pent-up frustration and unsaid grievances. Elliot fought the urge to lash out, knowing it would only undermine his argument. Instead, he took a deep breath, trying to suppress the rising tide of anger and despair. Rhys, who had been biting his tongue since taking his place at the table, finally snapped.

"Mr Huntingdon," the young miner said, "I implore you to reconsider your position. Put aside your objections for a moment. You have a moral obligation to us, the workers—to ensure our safety and well-being above all else. If you fail in this duty, you are no better than the ruthless mine owners of old, who treated their workers as expendable commodities. You may see us as uneducated oafs, but we know that you make a handsome profit from us thanks to the high demand for South Wales anthracite, the most prized premium coal there is. The rent we pay out of our meagre wages for our cottages goes straight into your coffers. Our scrip wage is spent in your general store. Surely there is some room for compromise. Investing in three additional ventilation shafts and installing upgraded fans is not an impossible feat, is it?"

"You need to listen to what Dr Blackwood has to say about ventilation," Elliot stated firmly. "Your senior engineer is convinced it could make a huge difference for us."

For a moment, there was silence, as Huntingdon's gaze locked onto Elliot's unwavering stare. Then, with a dismissive wave of his hand, the colliery owner replied.

"Your concerns have been noted, gentlemen, isn't that right, Dr Blackwood? However, I stand by my decision. Profits and pricing must come first if the mine is to continue to survive in such a competitive global market. Now, if there is no further business, I suggest we adjourn."

As the meeting ended, a growing sense of letdown and frustration settled upon the union workers. They were all too aware of the mine owner's greed and lack of concern for their well-being, having seen first-hand the suffering and loss endured by families in Cwmgryf and similar villages. The sight of Huntingdon's prized horses grazing on his manicured estate and pulling his freshly polished black carriage to the train station for his lavish parties in London was enough to make anyone seethe with anger. As they trudged out of the room, disheartened and enraged, they didn't realize that a glimmer of hope was landing in their lap.

Sitting steadfastly in his leather chair, the experienced engineer was meticulously perfecting his notes on the union's demands with his sharp insights. Each full-stop was marked with a forceful tap of his fountain pen's nib. As he continued to jot down more thoughts, his conviction seemed to bend his nib even all the more.

*

After many hours of hardening their battle plan at the Cwmgryf Working Men's Club, Elliot said his farewells to the trade union leaders. His furious expression wouldn't melt until he met his wife's gaze upon returning home as the pale moonlight enveloped the village.

Sitting in one of the worn armchairs, Ebba's face glowed with warmth and delight as she munched on another of the delicious gifted Welsh cakes, her stomach rumbling with hunger. Ebba held the still warm cake in her hands, feeling its gentle heat permeate her tired fingers. The door to the cottage swung open, revealing Elliot's tall figure silhouetted against the moonlit night outside. He paused for a moment, taking in the welcoming scene before him, and then crossed the room to join his wife.

He slumped into the worn-out armchair opposite, the day's fatigue finally catching up with him.

> "You look like you could use some cheering up," she said, offering him the last Welsh cake. "A treat from one of the families I helped today."

Feeling completely drained, the silence lingered between them. The only noise in the room came from the occasional crackle of the dying fire and the sound of their crumbs being brushed off their clothes.

"Today's been gruelling—," Elliot began, dragging a weary hand across his face. "Charles Huntingdon refused to listen to reason, dismissing our concerns about dire safety and working conditions. He spewed the same tired rhetoric about profitability ensuring job security. Things need shaking up. Politicians and their greedy colliery owner chums to be forced to see sense. They won't do it willingly. The unions must keep hammering for better conditions. It's working elsewhere. It can work here."

Ebba placed a hand on his arm, her touch gentle and reassuring.

The glowing, crackling fire danced across the walls of the snug cottage as they finished their dinner. Later, snuggled up together in bed, they entwined hands as they discussed their mission.

"As the protests across the country grow more and more chaotic, I can't help but worry about the possibility of things escalating too far here in Cwmgryf. Elliot, do you think the miner's will resort to striking?"

"Honestly, I'm not sure. But one thing's for certain—it's a difficult decision that shouldn't be taken lightly."

CHAPTER 6

Ebba Chadwick carefully examined the miner's chest with her cool stethoscope, listening intently to the persistent cough that had plagued him for months. A cloud of coal dust seemed to follow him into the clinic, settling on every surface and adding to the sombre atmosphere. With his head stuck in books for days, Elliot preferred to linger by her side, watching as his wife documented the man's condition and symptoms in a meticulous manner.

"Breathe out slowly, please, Dai. Long and slow. As smoothly as you can."

The man obliged, his breath hissing and bubbling as it escaped his chest and into the spirometer. Ebba looked at the reading and gave a silent, worried sigh.

"Thank you. That's all the tests done. I'll prescribe some medicine to help ease your cough and make it more productive," Ebba advised. "Now, I know you won't want to do this, but it's crucial that you wear your dust mask when working, if you want to stop any further deterioration in your breathing. Your lung capacity is severely compromised."

"Please don't think I am ungrateful, doctor, but wearing a mask for twelve hours as I labour away with my pickaxe just won't work. I'm a hewer. It's demanding work. Plus, the lads will tease me mercilessly. Proper men don't wear masks."

"Soon you won't be working at all, Dai, if the deterioration continues at this pace. You're a grown man and I can't tell you what to do. But if you don't actively take care of yourself, soon you'll be bedridden and you'll have no choice. I'll leave it up to your conscience."

Elliot carefully measured out the prescription, pouring a portion of the thick, brown liquid from a large glass flask into a smaller bottle for dispensing. Dai felt uncomfortable under Ebba's intense stare and nervously played with the cloth cap in his hands, avoiding eye contact.

"Cheers, doc," he mumbled as the bottle suddenly appeared in his view. "I'll be off then."

He groaned as he rose to his feet and went to leave, only to be almost knocked flying by an enthusiastic Gwen paying the doctors a visit.

"Blimey, sorry, Dai," she blurted out as she steadied the tired warrior of a man.

"I'd better get going to Cardiff, Ebba," said Elliot. "That report's not going to research itself. "

"Ebba, I've been thinking," Gwen blurted out as Ebba waved her husband off.

"Go on then, tell me. What bold scheme have you dreamed up this time."

"With all the good work we're doing here for the menfolk , perhaps we should also consider starting a special women's group meeting? The ladies of Cwmgryf could certainly benefit from having access to health education. Most of them still rely on an apple a day keeping the doctor away and not much else," Gwen sighed.

Ebba looked up from reviewing Dai's hurriedly scribbled notes. When her gaze met Gwen's determined expression, how could she ever refuse?

"Gwen, that's a wonderful idea—especially if the women are less proud and stubborn than their men! We might actually be able to talk some sense into them."

"Exactly!" Gwen giggled, her enthusiasm infectious. "And with my local connections and your medical expertise, we could make a real difference to these ladies. We could hold sessions on hygiene—even family planning. Think about it! No more huge families squashed into one room. Wave goodbye to unsanitary conditions at home."

"Easy there, Gwen! You'll cause a riot. Controlling fertility is going too far! Religious groups condemn any form of planning as interfering with

God's will, and society expects all women to embrace motherhood."

"But what about the women's rights movement?" Gwen said disappointedly. "Shouldn't a woman have control over her reproductive life? You're one of the few women I know who won't bow down to societal expectations," the midwife added, feeling her friend's disapproving gaze.

"One day at a time, Gwen," Elliot chimed in. "Let's focus on less contentious issues we can help with, like teaching them how to treat cuts, bruises, and burns."

"Well, the miners up in Derbyshire are striking for men's rights. What's wrong with standing up for women?"

Luckily, their argument was cut short by a disoriented cart boy who stumbled in, his forearm severely crushed.

*

The sun shone through the window of the local shop, casting its golden afternoon rays on Sian Williams as she restocked the shelves. Her heavily pregnant form made it tough for her to reach the top shelves, but she managed with a determined smile.

As she worked, thoughts of her husband Gethin filled her mind. She imagined him cradling their newborn with pride and love, his head tilted down just as he always did, his chocolate-brown hair falling over his eyes.

Just then, Gwen and Ebba walked into the shop, still talking about their debate over the women's clinic.

> "Hello, Sian. Here, let me help you with that," Gwen said warmly. "How are you feeling today?"

> "I'm doing well, thank you," Sian replied with a cheerful tone, though underlying anxiety could be heard. "But as you can see, it's getting harder to move around these days."

> "Do you want us to help?" Ebba offered.

> "That would be lovely, thank you."

As they assisted her, Sian shared her worries about her pregnancy. Being a first-time mother was overwhelming for her, and thinking about all the possible complications only added to her stress.

> "Dr Chadwick," Sian began hesitantly, "I've been having some pain in my lower back and I'm not sure if it's normal or something to worry about."

> "Let me have a look. Is that okay with you?"

Sian nodded nervously and stepped closer as Ebba pressed against her lumbar spine.

> "Does it hurt here?" Ebba asked.

> "Ouch. Yes!"

"There's no need to worry, Sian. It's completely normal for pregnant women to experience discomfort in their lower back, especially after being on their feet for a while like you've been. But if the pain becomes more intense or moves towards the front of your stomach, please come and see us. And don't forget, it's also natural to feel anxious about giving birth," Ebba reassured with a warm smile. "We're here to support you. Just try to relax a little."

"Thank you," Sian said with visible relief at the reassurance.

As the women continued their conversation, Bryn Jones stepped into the shop. His eyes narrowed when he spotted Ebba, and his resentment simmered beneath the surface. He approached the group, his stocky frame casting an imposing shadow.

"So, you are here meddling in Sian's life now? You think just because you're a doctor, you know what's best for everyone? I saw the Evans lad—his hand still all bandaged up and bloodied and it's ages since he got hurt."

Ebba maintained her composure, meeting Bryn's stare with a calm but firm response.

"Henry's wounds were quite severe and will take some weeks for his hand to fully heal. And although it's none of your business, I told him to come and see me to have his dressing changed if necessary, advice which he's clearly not followed. I'll pop over visit him later on today to give him a bit of extra help."

"Who says we need *'your'* help?" Bryn challenged, veins bulging on his neck.

Gwen stepped forward, her loyalty to Ebba evident.

"I do, Bryn. Dr Chadwick has been nothing but kind and helpful since she arrived. She's offering us all a chance for better healthcare thanks to working so hard with the Miner's Welfare Trust board, and I, for one, am grateful—for everything she does for us."

"Keep your opinions to yourself, Gwen!" Bryn snapped, even though the fire in his eyes had dimmed somewhat.

As he stomped off like a petulant toddler that didn't get its way, the tension dissipated, and Sian turned back to Gwen and Ebba.

"Thank you for your advice. It means everything. My Gethin can't wait to become a father to this one," she said lovingly cupping her belly.

"You'll make wonderful parents," Ebba trilled as the women picked up their provisions and headed to their respective homes, keen to enjoy a plate of good food, and a short break from the onslaught of cases they would need to face tomorrow.

Thirty miles away, the sun dipped below the horizon, the gas lamps now lighting the bustling streets of Cardiff. Inside the Miner's Institute, Elliot Chadwick's eyes scanned the pages of a dusty tome, deep in concentration. He had been researching tirelessly, trying to find any information that could help the trust improve the lives of their wards. As he leafed through the pages of one of the newspapers from the archive, he stumbled upon something that caught his attention: an article about the latest Coal Mines Act and its supposed shortcomings.

"By Jove," Elliot muttered quietly as he delved deeper into the information.

It was clear that decades of legislation were ineffective. Many politicians came from mine owners or were friends with industrialists needing cheap coal. The coal industry was highly skilled in lobbying for colliery owners' rights. The realisation there in black and white caused a surge of both anger and determination within him. What was the purpose of having laws if they couldn't protect innocent lives? In any civilised society, human lives *must* hold more value than this! Surely?

In a fit of rage, he slammed the large leather journal binder shut, causing a few heads to turn in the otherwise quiet reading room.

As the train rattled along the tracks, carrying him back home to Ebba, Elliot couldn't shake the thoughts swirling in his head. The injustice faced by the miners weighed heavily on his heart.

> "We must do something, my love. These miners deserve better than this."

Ebba listened intently to what he had found: the corruption, the institutional failures, the self-interested lobbying. Her eyes reflected the same mix of concern and determination that her husband felt.

> "You can't let this continue, Elliot. You have to reveal what you unearthed at the institute to the union representatives in the morning."

CHAPTER 7

The next day, Gwen Price stood in the dappled sunlight filtering through the stained glass windows of St David's Chapel, her hands clasped in anticipation as she waited for Reverend Thomas Jenkins.

> "Ah, Gwen, my dear, go on through to the vestry. I'll be with you in a jiffy," said the cleric, his silver hair catching the colourful light as he crossed the nave.
>
> "You're glowing with excitement! I assume you want to talk about your upcoming wedding?"
>
> "Yes. That's right. Take your time, I have a few minutes" she said, her voice trailing off as she turned into the tiny vestry.

Gwen's gaze traced round the room, looking intently at nothing in particular, until it landed on a letter protruding from an envelope on the reverend's desk.

The paper was crisp and white, and the neat cursive handwriting on the front was unmistakable. She couldn't resist a smile as she read the contents of the note.

> *'...and from this month donate 10 pounds a month of medical supplies to the new clinic, a cause close to my heart. However, due to personal*

circumstances, which I am sure you understand, this must remain our secret.'

Before she could tease the letter out and confirm her suspicions, the reverend breezed in, his cassock billowing behind him like a wizard's cape.

"As the good book says, 'love thy neighbour as thyself', and I can see that you and Llewellyn have truly taken this to heart. Your devotion to each other is a shining example for the rest of our village, and I pray that your bond will continue to strengthen with each passing day."

"Thank you, Reverend. Your support means the world to us. I know Llewellyn is often away at sea, but he does value your opinion. I wanted you to ask about our banns?"

"Don't worry about him being able to attend the readings. His captain can send a certificate with his intention to marry in lieu of that. What date did you have in mind?"

*

Ebba was taken aback by the success of the women's surgery open hour. Gwen was beaming as she showed Ebba a pile of thank-you notes from grateful patients.

"If we share these with the Trust, they'll have to see the value in what we're doing and allocate some budget for our cause, right?" Gwen asked eagerly.

Ebba grabbed one of the letters and began to read it aloud, her voice filled with pride.

> "I just hope the Trust sees it that way too, Gwen. There are so many other worthy causes competing for their support," she reflected, eyeing the dwindling supplies in the storeroom.

*

That evening, Ebba sat with Elliot by the fire, their minds far from their chaotic professional concerns for once. Elliot stroked the back of Ebba's hand as they shared stories of their day. Then a quiet moment fell between them, allowing their thoughts to wander towards their future. Ebba spoke first.

> "Elliot," she began hesitantly, her voice barely above a whisper, "do you ever think about— us? About having a child together, I mean?"

A delighted smile graced his lips and he leaned forward and gently stroked her face.

> "My darling, I truly believe that becoming parents would bring us immense joy. Perhaps in a year or two when things have calmed down here? Can you imagine how wonderful it will be?"

Elliot tugged at her hand and nodded to upstairs, but before they could ascend to the bedroom, their tender moment was interrupted by an insistent knock on the door. A distraught Mary Evans stood on the threshold, desperation etched on her face.

"Ebba, it's my Dai," she choked out, wringing her hands anxiously. "He hasn't been wanting to see you lately, but I can't bear to watch him suffer any longer. He's taken a turn for the worse. All he does is sleep. He won't eat or drink. I'm beside myself with worry. Please come and examine him—even if it means delivering bad news."

Ebba shared a worried glance with Elliot, then grabbed her coat, her warm maternal feelings swiftly replaced by a fierce determination to help.

CHAPTER 8

The steady drizzle pattered against the window of the cosy Evans' cottage. Elliot Chadwick stood beside his wife as she tended to Dai, once a robust man now reduced to a frail figure lying in bed, consumed by a relentless cough. His once muscular frame now nothing more than a shadow.

Ebba listened to his laboured breaths, her stethoscope skimming over his sunken chest, revealing only grim news. She glanced at the spirometer on the bedside table and knew that Dai was too weak to even attempt a reading.

> "His condition is deteriorating," Ebba whispered to Elliot, her voice barely audible over the rain and Dai's wheezing. "I'm afraid there's little else we can do for him except keep him comfortable."

Elliot nodded solemnly, his face reflecting the weight of his responsibilities and the heartache he felt for the Evans family. In the far corner of the room, Mary Evans wrung her hands together, her eyes a mixture of distress and anxiety as she watched the two doctors whispering, too heartbroken to approach the bed anymore. Her wiry hair was dishevelled, and her missing front tooth only added to her tired, battered and defeated appearance. She began to wail with sorrow.

"We'll do everything we can to ease his pain, Mary."

"Thank you, doctor," she replied, her voice cracking, as Dai drifted into a slumber again.

Aware of the enormity of responsibility resting on her shoulders, Mary Evans looked from her husband to their maimed son, Henry, sitting beside the fireplace in the small front room picking at his bandages wondering if his life would ever return to normal. Mary would soon be the head of a household with no income and no claim to the miner's accommodation that had been her home for three decades.

"Mary, I know this is difficult—Unfortunately, his black lung has advanced too far," Elliot said gently, trying to offer some comfort.

"Yer mean— there's no hope for 'im?" Mary asked, her voice barely a whisper. "He's bounced back before. Can't he—"

"I am afraid not. Not this time. Your husband has a few hours left at best. But Ebba and I are here to help him and support you in any way we can."

Mary nodded, tears welling up in her eyes. With a heavy heart, she took a deep breath and slowly reached out to touch Dai's hand. The gravity of the situation hung over them like a thick tarpaulin. Ebba could feel the tension in the room and offered to make the poor woman a cup of tea, hoping to provide some respite from her despair.

As she moved towards the stove, her mind raced with questions about whether she could have done more to save Dai. She knew black lung was ultimately fatal, but still, she had grown attached to the Evans family, and their pain felt like her own.

Water splashed beside the mug instead of in it as the door to Dai and Mary's cottage burst open, slamming against the wall with a resounding crack. Bryn Jones and his wife, known as the 'wise woman of the valley', stormed in with faces contorted with rage. The atmosphere in the room turned as cold as the draught they brought with them.

"Oi, missus!" Bryn barked, jabbing a thick finger at Ebba.

"You ain't done enough for Dai! It's your fault he's sufferin' like this! My Bess should be looking after him."

Bess stood beside the ogre, arms crossed, her eyes narrowed in agreement. She clutched a bundle of dried herbs and roots, ready to take over Dai's care with her traditional remedies.

"Bryn," Elliot said, stepping forward to defuse the situation, "Ebba has been doing everything she can for Dai. We both have."

"Have you though? Why should I trust a Sheehan?" Barney spat, brandishing a yellowed newspaper clipping. "I was clearing out the

Working Men's Club storeroom when I found this—front page news about Elijah Sheehan being hanged for murder! Well Bess and I kept reading and found out he was survived by a daughter, Ebba. There aren't many female doctors, so after digging a bit more, we discovered another paper mentioning 'Ebba Sheehan'. Considering how quickly Dai's condition has declined, how can we know you're not as sick as your father? That poor Mrs Iverson was murdered in cold blood."

Ebba was stunned, her face a mix of shock and confusion. Her heart raced as the past she had worked so hard to bury resurfaced once again. She knew that her connection to Elijah Sheehan could ruin her reputation in the community if it ever came out, but she never expected it to happen like this.

"Bryn," she pleaded, trying to reason with him while Mary Evans stood by, mouth agape. "My father's actions have nothing to do with my abilities as a doctor. I had little contact with him throughout my life. And these medicines are widely respected for their safety and effectiveness—"

The beast was about to launch another attack on Ebba when her husband cut him down to size.

"Enough!" Elliot yelled, with a thuggish tone. "Your wife's herbal remedies won't save Dai, Mr Jones. His condition is too advanced. This isn't the first time you've seen black lung take a man in his prime. We're all doing our best for him. Your yelling and stomping is upsetting Mrs Evans and Henry and not helping Dai at all. Show some decorum, man!"

Coming to her senses, Mary Evans stepped forward to defend Ebba.

"Bryn, please, I know you are like a brother to him," she pleaded, her voice cracking with emotion, "but you must understand that Ebba's been doing everything she can for Dai. This terrible illness. It's beyond any of our control."

Bryn's face softened ever so slightly as he looked back at his old pal, head lolling, chest heaving, yet his anger and grief still simmered just beneath the surface. He knew full well that no amount of Bess's herbal remedies could save his friend, but the pain and fear had made him desperate for someone to blame—and that blame fell squarely onto Ebba.

"Ya better be telling me the truth, Mary," Jones grumbled, giving Ebba one last accusatory glare.

"Bryn," Mary continued, her voice stronger now. "You know as well as I do that if there was a chance to save Dai, Ebba would have done it. She cares deeply for all of us in this village. Don't punish her for something she didn't cause and don't let old rumours cloud your judgment. I'd thank you to leave our house and let Dai have some rest!"

Irritated and frustrated, the bully spun around and marched out of the cottage, dragging his wife and her bundle of herbs with him. The commotion caught the attention of nosy neighbours, who had been eavesdropping at their doors and peeking through tattered curtains to catch every detail, every word, and every aggressive gesture.

Ebba stood up as the door slammed behind them, her heart still pounding. Despite Mary and Elliot's comforting presence, her anguish remained. She knew the news of her father's crimes would surely spread, undermining everything she was working so hard to achieve. It was a familiar feeling, one she had first experienced in London a decade ago when her father, Elijah, was arrested and found guilty of murder. Now, the treacherous rumours threatened to swirl again around Cwmgryf. Ebba couldn't ignore the feeling that history was repeating itself. She knew Bryn would stop at nothing to discredit her, just like last time. The familiar sense of powerlessness washed over her, as she braced herself for another onslaught of gossip from anonymous sources. Would she ever escape the relentless judgment that seemed to follow her wherever she went?

"That man will not break me," she declared fiercely to Elliot, her eyes blazing with determination. "I will continue to stand up for this community, even if it means fighting harder than ever before."

"I'll be by your side every step of the way. You can count on that."

Elliot returned her determined gaze with a faint smile, though deep inside he couldn't shake his fear of what might happen next. The Evans' cottage fell into an uneasy silence, tension and fear hanging in the air.

Mary gripped her husband's frail hand with all her strength, preparing herself for the impending wave of sorrow that would inevitably engulf her. Henry stood silently behind his mother, his one good hand resting lightly on her shoulder. He felt consumed by guilt, utterly powerless. Together, they braced themselves for the heart-wrenching loss that was about to haunt them forever.

CHAPTER 9

With the memory of Bryn's accusations still ringing in her ears, Ebba felt a weight settle upon her chest, heavy as the miner's lung that plagued Dai. She watched as he took each laboured breath and wondered if she had indeed done *everything* she could for him and his family.

"Everything alright, Ebba?" Elliot asked gently, placing a reassuring hand on her shoulder. His touch was warm, but it did little to dispel the chill of doubt creeping into her heart.

"Is there really nothing more we can do?" she whispered, her eyes never leaving Dai's gaunt face.

"Darling, you've been doing your best. You know as well as I do black lung is terminal. It was already very advanced before you even met him," Elliot replied softly. "Dai's condition is beyond our control. As Mary says he's in God's hands now. You can't blame yourself for the progression of his illness. It's been building for years."

Despite his comforting words, a nagging uncertainty remained within Ebba. As a doctor, she knew the limitations of medicine and the inevitability of death—but as a woman who had fought hard to gain trust and respect from the villagers, she couldn't help but wonder if she had somehow failed them.

Within the hour, poor old Dai Evans had breathed his last. Mary's head lay sobbing on his still chest.

*

The next day, a sombre atmosphere hung over the village as news of beloved Dai Evans' passing spread. Widow Mary was inconsolable, mourning the loss of her devoted husband of thirty years. Rhys worked quietly on a rough wooden cross to mark Dai's final resting place in a pauper's grave.

Ebba couldn't help but feel overwhelmed with guilt and regret as she watched the funeral procession wind its way through the village. She could sense the accusatory stares of many, blaming her for Dai's death. Bryn's glares burned into her back as he marched along, his anger and bitterness towards Ebba evident.

But among the disapproving looks and murmurs, there were those who stood by Ebba's side—Elliot, Gwen, and the Reverend. They knew the truth— that Ebba had given Dai the best care possible—but it did little to ease her troubled heart.

As they laid Dai to rest, Ebba desperately tried not to weep as she grappled with crushing feelings of failure, doubt and injustice.

Lost in her thoughts, vision blurred with tears, she didn't see one of the mourners offer words of comfort to Mary and discreetly slip her a small envelope from a coat pocket.

"If there's anything at all, Mary," the mourner said, their voice steady and reassuring, "we're here for you."

CHAPTER 10

Later that day, Ebba sat alone at her dining table, simmering with anger towards Bryn Jones. *How dare he accuse me when he knows nothing about medicine?* She thought bitterly over her cup of tea. *'I didn't even make his tincture, Elliot did. It was the black lung that killed him. Years spent down in the colliery did him in. Not me.'*

She gazed out the window, taking in the faint lights from a long row of cottages, one of which belonged to Mary Evans, who was probably still sobbing and clutching onto her late husband's old cloth cap.

After the tense feud with Bryn Jones, a change came over the people of Cwmgryf. Whispers and sideways glances followed Ebba as she went about her business and suspicion weighed heavily on her conscience. But Ebba remained strong, standing firm against the cowardly accusations and unwarranted doubts. She refused to let these crushing opinions get her down.

After the tense feud with Barney Jones, a change came over the people of Cwmgryf. Whispers and sideways glances followed Ebba as she went about her tasks, suspicion casting a long shadow over her. But Ebba refused to be cowed. She met every unspoken accusation and unwarranted doubt with unwavering resolve, determined not to let the weight of their opinions crush her spirit.

Ebba strolled down the quiet High Street, the cool autumn breeze rustling her hair and sending a shiver down her spine. It was undeniable. The once welcoming village had lost its sparkle, replaced by an air of suspicion and mistrust that seemed to linger over the cobbled streets and grubby whitewashed cottages. As she walked past the local shops, snippets of hushed conversations reached her ears.

> "Did you hear about that Chadwick woman? Her old man was the killer, Elijah Sheehan," one lass whispered to another as they stood chin wagging the butcher's.
>
> "Can't trust someone like that," a bloke grumbled, leaning against the wall near the grocers. "The apple doesn't fall far from the tree, eh? Her pa killed a woman cold-blooded like a farmer slits the throat of a fattened pig. Who knows what she could do?"
>
> "Such a pity, really," chimed in an older woman, on her way to chapel to arrange the flowers for Sunday's service. "She seemed like such a sweet thing. But now with these rumours—"

As the hours passed, Ebba's heart sank as more voices blended into an unsettling cacophony. Still determined to gather supplies for Elliot's meal, Ebba stepped into the grocers where Sian Williams, the loyal mother-to-be, greeted her with a sympathetic look.

"Oh Ebba," Sian said softly, noting the worry on Ebba's exhausted face. "I've heard people talking, you know. About your father. The village talks about nothing else to be honest. I'm so sorry."

A pang of hurt and injustice shot through Ebba, but she mustered a brave smile anyway.

"I suspected as much, Sian. I plan to address these rumours tomorrow evening on the village green, call a meeting where they hold the miners' union addresses. Will you stand by me?"

"Of course," Sian replied, her voice resolute. "You've been nothing but kind and dedicated to this community. It's so unfair for people to judge you based on your father's actions that were from years ago—especially a father who abandoned you to die on the streets! I think you've suffered enough. It's time for this nonsense to stop. Gethin's fuming about it, but he doesn't say anything publicly—there's just too many doubters. I wish we could do more."

"Thank you for your honesty and your support," Ebba whispered, blinking back tears of gratitude.

Her spirits lifted, a newfound determination taking root.

Leaving the shop with her things for supper, she stepped back onto the street with a renewed sense of purpose. *'You will not ruin my future twice, Elijah*

Sheehan,' she vowed silently, her chin lifting with defiance.

*

That evening as she sat by the fire, with Elliot reading his research paper for the Trust, Ebba poured her heart into crafting a speech that would lay bare her past and demonstrate her unwavering determination to serve the people of Cwmgryf. She would not allow her father's sins to overshadow her own good deeds and dedication ever again. The villagers deserved the truth, and good care, and she would give both to them until her last breath.

The following day, word spread quickly through the village of Ebba's impending address on the village green. As the sun set over to the west, a large crowd gathered, curiosity, cruelty and caution mingling in the air. Ebba stood tall and took a deep breath.

As the trailblazing female doctor's voice sliced through the murmuring hostile crowd, she saw curiosity turn to attention and many of the most judgmental eyes begin to soften.

> "Many years ago, my feckless Irish father was a carpenter in London," she declared with unflinching resolve. "Driven by selfishness he drove a wedge between Mrs Iverson and her husband, for his own financial gain. His murderous actions caused irreparable harm to

that family, and for that, I am deeply sorry. But let it be known—I played no part in his deeds. I was but a child, left behind when he selfishly abandoned me well before my eighth birthday. I cannot be sure as he also abandoned my mother who died soon after."

She paused, her chest heaving as she collected herself with some deep breaths before tackling the swirling rumours head-on.

"As well as tarring me with the same brush as my father, many of you have questioned my medical qualifications and speculated about my intentions here in the village. Let me be clear: My father's past does not define my present or future. I have fought tooth and nail to earn my place as one of the first women on the highly esteemed General Medical Council, despite more obstacles and prejudice than I care to remember. Being a doctor isn't just my profession. It's my life's calling. All I live for is to heal, not harm."

A murmur swept through the gathered crowd, accompanied by nodding heads and disapproving frowns from the naysayers. A few disgruntled villagers stormed off, their hearts too hardened against Ebba and her presence. But this only fuelled her determination more.

"And above all," Ebba's voice rang out, her gaze sweeping across the faces before her, "I stand before you not just as a doctor, but as a woman dedicated to this community. My clinic doors are open to all, whatever your class. I will fight for you. My husband champions your rights on the Miner's Benevolent Trust board, and takes your concerns and grievances directly to Mr Huntingdon. Just as the Salvation Army, the family that embraced me when my own father left me for dead, opened their hearts to me, so too will I open mine to you. I swear to you now, I will not rest until every single soul in Cwmgryf receives the care and support they deserve."

Every word dripped with sincerity and conviction. She had laid her soul bare for all to see.

"And finally," she proclaimed, "I extend my deepest gratitude to those who have stood by me through these tumultuous times—my husband Dr Chadwick, my steadfast colleague Miss Price, and loyal friends Mr and Mrs Gethin Williams. Your unwavering support has been my anchor as my world has threatened to fall apart."

A few people started to clap, then most of the crowd erupted in applause. The angriest marched off: turning them would take longer, but she was determined to do it.

As the crowd began to disperse, Ebba sensed a renewed flicker of hope igniting within her. It was then, the warm smiles of Elliot, Gwen, Gethin, and Sian came into focus. Through sheer honesty and relentless determination, perhaps she could finally break free from the shadow of her father's crimes once and for all and rebuild the trust she richly deserved.

Gwen and Elliot approached.

> "You were amazing up there," Gwen chirped. "Don't worry about those few who walked off. They will come around eventually. Sometimes you have to accept how things are, no matter how unfair it feels, else it eats into you. Give them time. And you. They'll come around."

Ebba let out a sigh of relief. The support meant everything to her.

> "We'll always stand by you," Gethin said.

> "It's just so difficult to shake off this feeling of betrayal," she confessed, wiping away a stray tear.

Gwen put a comforting arm around her friend.

> "I know it hurts, but don't let it consume you. Your actions will speak louder than any false accusations or rumours."

Ebba nodded, taking comfort in Gwen's wise words, but not fully agreeing with them. She had put everything on the line for the chance to help the people of the village, yet some still saw her only as the daughter of a criminal.

As Ebba made her way home with Elliot by her side, she couldn't hold back the tears any longer. Elliot wrapped a strong arm around her shoulders, offering silent support as they went inside and gladly shut out the turbulent world behind them.

> "Why does my horrid father's past still have power over me? It feels so unfair," Ebba asked through sobs as she struggled to hang up her coat.

Elliot stopped and turned to face her, gently cupping her face in his hands.

> "It's because he was your father, connected to you by blood," he said, his voice full of empathy. "And no matter how much we try to distance ourselves from our past, for most people, rightly or wrongly, our family will always be a part of us and how we are perceived."

Ebba sighed deeply and felt the warmth of Elliot's hand on her tear-stained cheek. She longed for the comfort and strength that his presence brought her.

> "I just wish I could escape it entirely," she admitted, her voice quivering with emotion.

Elliot's embrace grew tighter around her waist as he drew her in closer.

> "You can't control how others perceive you," he reminded her gently. "But what truly matters is

how you see yourself. And from my perspective, I see a resilient, kind-hearted woman who has triumphed over countless challenges."

A small smile graced Ebba's lips as Elliot's shared his kind words, and he planted a loving kiss on them.

In that moment, she wished for time to freeze so she could hold onto this feeling of acceptance and understanding forever. Lately, she had been so exhausted from putting on her cheerful bedside manner, but with Elliot by her side in that moment, she felt truly understood.

"Come on, Ebba, love. Let's turn in. Tomorrow's a new day."

CHAPTER 11

In the following days a more cheerful and resilient Ebba Chadwick stood in the small, cluttered storeroom of the modest clinic, her hands on her hips as she surveyed the shelves packed with a fresh delivery of medical supplies and equipment.

Her heart had swelled with gratitude at the sudden arrival of the much-needed aid from the Trust, along with an unexpected second delivery of more basics like slings, splints, antiseptic cream and bandages that would make a significant difference to the struggling miners and their families in Cwmgryf.

The cruel gossip that had plagued her and her husband in recent weeks seemed to have abated for now, allowing them to focus on their core mission: providing care and support to the community, and not being distracted by cruel jibes.

> "Please thank the Trust for this latest delivery, Elliot," Ebba called out to her husband who was holed up in the tiny consulting room, frantically arranging seats for a surprise delegation from the miners' charity. "We'll be able to help so many more people now that these new supplies have arrived."

"Indeed," he replied, his voice slightly muffled through the thin walls. "Now, gentlemen, let's begin."

Half an hour later, a group of miners dropped by, standing respectfully holding their cloth caps.

"Dr Ebba?"

"And what can I do for you?" she greeted cheerfully.

"Excuse me, ma'am. We've come to talk to your husband about the mine's safety measures," Tom Watts said anxiously, glancing at Ebba and her husband's closed door. "We heard there's important visitors from the Trust here because of the poor safety conditions and practices. Even basic equipment like Davy lamps are missing for many workers. We fear a disaster is looming. Mr Huntingdon and his men refuse to address it. Please, we're desperate."

Ebba's heart lurched at their words, a chill creeping up her spine. She knew all too well just how many British mining communities lived in fear of another deadly tragedy, with horrifying statistics from recent newspapers showing that hundreds of miners were killed and thousands more injured in explosions, floods, and collapses annually.

The constant threat weighed heavily on everyone's minds, especially given Huntingdon's disinterested, selfish attitude and woeful lack of inclination to improve worker welfare.

"Can we come in?" she enquired as her husband's conversation with the Trust representatives was drawing to a close.

As the men filed in, their heavy hobnail boots clomping on the bare floorboards. Ebba glanced at Elliot, her eyes conveying the gravity of the situation.

"Dr Chadwick, we need your help," Tom continued. "We're worried about the safety of our lads down in the pits. The wooden supports for the deeper seams are simply too weak, and there's been talk of the faint smell of gas. There's not enough lamps, and deadly coal dust hanging in the air, clogging up our lungs. We've raised our concerns with Gerald Price, the foreman, time and time again, but he dismisses us as troublemakers."

"I understand, gentlemen. The Trust is aware of these valid concerns and is addressing them with the mine owner and his senior engineer."

"I don't mean to sound rude or ungrateful, Doctor. But words alone won't suffice. Men's lives are at risk here and we need immediate action. Strike action."

"Gentlemen, I beg of you to consider a strong, diplomatic approach to this terrible situation," Reverend Jenkins advised.

"As you all know, resorting to a strike should only be done as a last resort, after exhausting all other options. The consequences of such an action will not just impact you, but your families as well. Is that truly what you wish for?"

The miners shifted uncomfortably, their expressions mirroring the weight of the reverend's words. Many had witnessed the devastating effects of past strikes in the country, and the memories of hardship, hunger, and despair were still all too fresh in their minds.

"Remember, when you strike, Huntingdon holds the power to evict you and your loved ones from your homes," Reverend Jenkins continued, his voice tinged with a solemn warning. "A man as ruthless as him won't hesitate to bring in blacklegs to replace you, ensuring that you never set foot in another mine in this valley. Is that truly the bleak future you desire for yourselves and your loved ones?"

The room fell silent, the men contemplating the gravity of their decision.

"I urge you to consider the path of diplomacy, as we are doing," Elliot implored, his eyes meeting those of the miners. "We shall engage in discussions with Huntingdon, present your grievances, and seek a resolution that benefits all parties involved. It is through open communication and understanding that we can hope to achieve lasting change."

"I suppose you have a point," Tom moaned. "We'll take your lead. But you need to understand we're tired of being treated like cattle and Charles Huntingdon needs to show us some respect. And soon."

None of them realised that the time for diplomacy was slipping away with each tick of the clock. Unbeknownst to them, a storm was gathering on the horizon, a tempest that threatened to engulf Cwmgryf Colliery and all those who relied on it.

.

CHAPTER 12

A deafening roar ripped through the valley, shaking the very foundations of the cottage. Windows rattled violently in their frames, a spiderweb of cracks splintering across one pane. Ebba's enamel mug danced along the table, then tumbled onto the floor splashing its contents over the floorboards. Her heart hammered in her chest at her terrible realisation: the explosion had come from the mine.

"Elliot!" she screamed, the name tearing from her throat.

Her husband jumped to his feet without hesitation. He grabbed his great coat, quickly kissing Ebba's pale lips before joining the army of men rushing towards the colliery, filled with an instinctive terror to flee and a duty to take action. In the distance, a thick plume of dark smoke clawed at the sky, a haunting reminder of the imminent danger that awaited them. Lit by the fiery glow of the burning mine, the men's reddened faces were grim and filled with dread. Each pounding step, each ragged breath, was a race against time to save the lives that hung in the balance.

"Be safe, my love," Ebba whispered as she threw bandages, slings and splints into her black leather bag and followed in the men's wake. *'Elliot! Please—please—stay away from the mine.'*

As they rushed towards the colliery, Elliot couldn't help but recall the miners' warnings about the dangerous conditions. All of their worst fears had become a reality due to failed attempts at negotiation, and now countless lives were in danger.

With the rescue team assembled, a group of banksmen frantically doused the remaining flames with buckets of water. The acrid smell of smoke and scorched wood filled the air, a grim reminder of the danger they were in. Elliot Chadwick, his heart pounding in his chest, took a deep breath and steeled himself for the daunting task ahead. He knew their chances were slim, but he was determined to save as many lives as possible. Giving a final nod to his fellow rescuers, Elliot joined the tail end of the line as they marched resolutely towards the lift cages that would transport them down the shaft to the pit head, ready to face the unknown depths and darkness that lay within.

Ebba watched from the colliery gates as Elliot and the other men disappeared from view. Her heart pounded in her chest. She knew Elliot was brave and capable, but she couldn't shake the sickening thought that he would not return. He was a bookworm not a collier. Studying mining textbooks was no match for the true experiences of working underground, but his kind heart always led him into perilous situations.

From the relative safety of the pit's delivery yard, Ebba saw the whole community thrust into a whirlwind of activity. Men who were off shift dashed back and forth carrying their colleagues, brought on stretchers from below, to safety. Others, terrified by the ordeal, sought comfort in one another's arms. The air was heavy with shock, the explosion having ripped through the morning tranquillity like a scythe harvesting wheat.

"Dr Chadwick!" A woman's panicked voice cut through the chaos, jolting Ebba into action. "We need your help! There's loads of injured blokes coming , like this one over here! Please!"

"Certainly, Mrs Griffiths," Ebba responded, her professional instincts kicking in amidst the devastation, desperately rummaging in her medical bag as she followed the woman.

The scene was chaotic. Frantic family members tended to bloodied and battered miners. The young doctor moved from patient to patient, her hands working quickly and efficiently as she assessed and prioritised the casualties and administered treatment to those in greatest need. Yet, her mind never strayed far from Elliot and the rescue team, constantly worrying about their safety.

"Dr Chadwick! My husband's still down there!" a distraught woman wailed, clutching Ebba's arm with desperate strength. "How long will he last? Please, tell me!"

"The rescuers are doing everything they can," Ebba said, trying to hide her voice trembling. "We have to trust them to do their job."

Meanwhile, deep in the mine's suffocating blackness, Elliot and his fellow rescuers battled against seemingly insurmountable odds. The tunnels, a treacherous labyrinth of twisted metal and shattered rock, threatened to collapse at any moment. The ever-present danger of poisonous gas hung heavy in every alcove. Yet, undeterred, the men forged ahead, fuelled by their training and unyielding determination to reach their trapped brethren.

> "Over here!" one of the rescuers called out, his voice muffled by the thick choking dust. "I've found someone!"

The men converged on the spot, carefully lifting the injured miner from the wreckage and carrying him back towards the lift shaft. It was a small victory, but each life saved fuelled their determination to delve deeper into the mine, trying not to think about the increased danger.

Back at the delivery yard, Ebba wiped sweat from her brow as she finished cleaning and stitching a miner's thigh wound. Her hands were slick with dark, caked blood, but she barely noticed. Her beloved Elliot, who had bravely vanished into the mine's depths some time ago, remained unaccounted for.

Sian's hands shook as she clutched the front of her frock, knuckles pale with tension. Her heavily pregnant figure swayed slightly on the doorstep of her little cottage, gazing out at the pandemonium unfolding before her. The pungent smell of smoke and distant shouts of panic filled the air, but like Ebba, her mind was consumed by one thought: was her husband trapped in the mine?

"Mrs Williams," a voice broke through her reverie.

It was Elsie from next door, her face etched with concern.

"Have you heard anything about your Gethin?"

Sian shook her head, tears welling up in her eyes.

"Well then, come now, dear," Elsie said gently, taking Sian's arm. "Watch your step. There we go. Let's see if we can find out what's going on. I'm sure you'll be with your Gethin soon."

Together, they joined the throngs of villagers making their way towards the mine, carrying blankets, food, and water to those emerging from the wreckage. Others, their faces etched with fear and desperation, formed little circles, their voices a collective plea for divine intervention.

"Please let him be safe," Sian murmured, as her eyes desperately searched the faces of the survivors for any sign of Gethin.

Her tortured mind raced, contemplating the horrifying prospect of raising their child alone, without the man she had loved.

A sudden shout drew everyone's attention back to the mine entrance. One group of rescuers, their faces blackened with soot and sweat, stumbled out into the daylight, several miners clinging to them for support. The crowd let out a collective sigh of relief, but it was short-lived as the ground trembled again.

"Get back!" one of the rescuers shouted, his voice hoarse and strained. "It could–"

Before he could even finish his warning, a smaller explosion boomed from the mine, shooting up a cloud of dust and smoke. The crowd gasped in terror, some bursting into tears while others stood frozen, unable to process the hellish scene unfolding before them.

"God help us," Sian whispered, her heart sinking as she clutched her belly.

She couldn't shake the feeling that her husband was still in there, stuck in the black void with death creeping closer and closer.

"Stay strong, my dear," Elsie murmured, squeezing Sian's hand. "Miracles can happen. We mustn't lose hope."

As the rescuers regrouped and courageously went on another sortie, Sian joined Ebba in praying for their husbands' safe return.

The coal mine was pitch black, illuminated only by the flickering light of Davy lamps. Rhys and Owen Davies were at the front, their faces set in a determined expression as they led the rescue team. Elliot and Reverend

Jenkins struggled to keep up with the experienced miners. The reverend clutched his Bible tightly, whispering prayers under his breath.

> "Look out!" Owen shouted, his arm outstretched to halt the team as the ground groaned ominously beneath them.

The floor ahead had collapsed, revealing a gaping chasm that plunged into the darkness below, exposing the full extent of the devastation. Reverend Jenkins gasped, his eyes widening in horror as he peered into the abyss.

> "The merciful Lord will guide us," the cleric whispered, his voice strained with fear.

> "Hey! Shh! Over there!" Bryn Jones's voice hissed. "Do you hear that?"

The rescuers moved cautiously, hearts pounding in their chests, hoping against hope that they would find someone alive.

As they rounded a corner, they came upon a small group of miners huddled together, their faces streaked with dirt and tears. One of them, a young lad no older than fourteen, was cradling the limp body of a fellow miner in his arms, his thin frame wracked with sobs.

> "We're here to help," Reverend Jenkins said, rushing forward to offer solace and support.

> "Too late for him," the boy choked out between sobs. "But there's others still trapped further in."

"Take heart, boyo," Bryn said, his voice surprisingly gentle. "We'll get 'em out, you hear?"

The rescue team pushed on, leaving the survivors in the care of another group who had joined them. The air became increasingly putrid as they delved further into the mine, every breath a struggle. Elliot's chest was hot and constricted, but he refused to let his body betray him.

"Please, Lord, protect these brave men," Reverend Jenkins prayed quietly, sweat gathering on his forehead. "Lead us to those still lost in this darkness."

"We'll make Huntingdon pay for this," warned Bryn and for once everyone agreed with him.

"Shh! What's that," said Owen.

A low moan echoed through the tunnel, and the rescue team sprang into action. They found another miner pinned beneath a fallen beam, his face wracked with pain. With a collective heave, they managed to free him. Reverend Jenkins offered soothing words as they hoisted his broken body onto a makeshift stretcher.

"Thank you," the injured man rasped, his eyes filling with tears. "God bless you all."

"Stay strong, friend," Elliot said, his hand placed firmly on the man's shoulder. "We won't leave you behind."

As they continued their search, the oppressive darkness and stifling air weighed heavily on their spirits, exhaustion threatening to extinguish their resolve. But with each survivor brought to safety, a flicker of hope reignited, spurring them onward.

But for every life they rescued, there were others that slipped through their grasp—still, silent bodies that would forever serve as a haunting reminder of the cruel fate that befell so many of those who worked in the mines.

> "May their souls find peace," Reverend Jenkins murmured over the bodies they discovered, his voice thick with sorrow.

Bryn's jaw clenched, his fists trembling with barely-contained rage at the senseless loss of life.

> "Come on, let's keep going," Elliot spluttered, his voice almost gone. "The tally board says there are still at least a dozen more to find."

In his eagerness to save more souls, Elliot turned down another passageway, unaware that he had become separated from the others. He called out until his voice was raw and hoarse, but only the oppressive silence of the pit answered. Panic rising in his chest, he desperately hammered the heel of his boot against the pit walls, but the sound was swallowed by the groaning and creaking of the unstable mineshafts.

*

Soon, the first glimmers of sunlight pierced through the smoky haze that still hung over the mine entrance, casting a hopeful glow on the crowd of anxious faces gathered there. A murmur of anticipation rippled through the assembly as one by one, the rescue team emerged from the depths, guiding weary and dishevelled survivors to safety. Cheers and sobs of relief filled the air as family members embraced their loved ones, their gratitude plain to see as they clung to each other.

> "Thank God you're alright!" cried Elsie, her arms wrapped tightly around her husband's staggering soot-streaked form. I've been praying for you all night".
>
> "Your prayers have been answered, Elsie," Reverend Jenkins said gently, his hands making a sign of the cross. "Our Lord has been merciful for you today."

As the village exhaled a collective sigh of relief, Ebba Chadwick stood apart from the jubilant crowd, her belly churning with dread. With each passing moment, her worry for Elliot intensified, gnawing at her like a starving beast. Each time a rescue team emerged from the mine, her eyes frantically scanned their faces, but Elliot was nowhere to be found. The grim expressions of the returning men confirmed her worst fears. Though each assumed he was with another crew, a bone-chilling certainty gripped Ebba's heart: something was terribly wrong.

"Elliot?" she called out, her voice barely a whisper as panic threatened to overwhelm her. "Has anyone seen my husband?"

"Dr Chadwick?" Tom Watts asked as he approached her, concern furrowing his brow. "I'm sorry, ma'am. We haven't seen him come out yet."

Ebba's voice trembled with desperation as she pleaded, her eyes full of tears.

"Please, you have to find him. I can't bear the thought of losing him."

Tom grasped her hand firmly and reassured her.

"We will do everything in our power to find Elliot. He's one of us! We would never leave him behind."

As the search for Elliot continued, Ebba paced anxiously, her mind consumed with worries and unspoken thoughts. Meanwhile, Sian, who was just weeks away from giving birth and unable to move much, sat on a delivery crate wrapped in a worn blanket. She watched the constant activity around her, silently praying for Gethin to return safely. Her hands were tightly clasped together as she begged God to bring her husband back.

An hour later, Ebba saw a body lifted onto a stretcher, its face covered with a sack. In blind panic, she ran over and yanked away the cloth. A face she knew well stared back at her—Gethin Williams. She gently closed his eyes and replaced the cloth, then made the slow painful walk to Sian.

The expectant mother's wailing filled the dark, smoky air, as her heart broke into a thousand pieces. Seeing Sian so distraught, Ebba wondered how she was going to react to bad news about Elliot. It seemed too impossible to even contemplate, and though she was never superstitious, for some reason she didn't want to tempt fate that day.

As the sun rose over the Welsh hills, Ebba stood watch. Her heart was heavy and she held her breath in anticipation. The growing light revealed the dirty faces of those emerging from the mine, their blank expressions a stark contrast to the fresh start to the day.

Surely someone must know something about Elliot by now?

CHAPTER 13

As dawn fully arrived, a weary yet victorious Elliot emerged from the mine. The villagers let out a collective gasp at the sight of him, followed by a wave of relief and gratitude that spread through the crowd like cool refreshing water on parched soil.

"Oi, Ebba! Wake up!" yelled Tom, giving the dozing woman a shake. "He's alive! Elliot's back! Quick!"

She leapt up and rushed to the shambolic figure hobbling towards her.

"Thank goodness you're all right!" She exclaimed, tears prickling her eyes as she buried her face in the curve of his neck. "I'll have no arguments. You need to go to bed and rest. You've been through so much. What were you thinking getting involved in that rescue? We needed you just as much here on the surface."

"My remit here is to protect these men, no matter what. Anyway, there's no time for debate, we need to get to the clinic and help Gwen. People need our help," he croaked.

His face was smudged with soot and dirt, but his eyes blazed with fierce determination. The weary doctor motioned for one of the lads with a pony and cart to take them to the clinic. As the cart bumped along the cobbled road, Elliot's thoughts raced with the recent events: the loss of lives and those still trapped underground. It weighed heavily on his heart.

*

"Thank goodness you're here!" groaned Gwen, the moment they walked in. "You won't believe the night I've had. Thankfully, a few of the village women who came to our open hour volunteered to help."

In the moments that followed, the midwife bustled from bed to bed, making sure to tend to the most severe injuries first. She relayed the pertinent details of each case to the tired doctors, apologising for not being able to complete meticulous patient notes as usual.

"Don't worry Gwen, we'll take it from here. You should head home and rest," Ebba said.

With relief, the exhausted midwife picked up her coat, and dashed back to her simple lodgings with Uncle Ifan in double quick time.

*

The dull grey sky loomed as the community gathered for the memorial service of the twenty-three lives lost in the explosion. Ebba stood by Elliot, their arms linked, facing the grieving crowd united. It all seemed so senseless. Why did another tragedy have to occur?

"Dear friends," began Reverend Jenkins, his voice crisp and confident, "we have come together to mourn the loss of our brothers, sons, and fathers who perished in the terrible explosion yesterday at the colliery."

"Let us never forget the sacrifices they made in their quest for the precious black gold that fuels our nation and powers our empire, harvested from beneath these verdant hills," he continued, his voice thick with emotion as tears and sniffles echoed around him. "And may we find the strength to honour their memories by working tirelessly for a safer future for all those who toil underground. Let us also remember to support the widows and children left behind, whose lives have been shattered by this disaster. Look out for your neighbours. As we lay our dearly departed brothers to rest, let us not only honour their sacrifice, but also remember the solace and assistance they have helped provide to their loved ones through their contributions to the miners' fund."

At the far edge of the churchyard, a gaping pit had been dug, a grim testament to the mine's devastating death toll. Twenty-three lifeless bodies, carefully wrapped in shrouds and lovingly placed within, now lay together in this makeshift communal tomb. As Reverend Jenkins spoke words of comfort and scripture, each mourner laid a flower or ribbon atop the mound of earth.

The reverend's words echoed across the gathering:

"The Lord is my shepherd, I shall not want.

He maketh me to lie down in green pastures: he leadeth me beside the still waters. He restoreth my soul—"

But this was not merely a moment of mourning. It was a call to action, a rallying cry for change. The tragedy that had befallen these men served as a stark reminder of the dangers they faced each day in the unforgiving depths of the mine.

As the villagers bowed their heads in prayer, a fire of determination ignited within their hearts. The fight for justice, for safer working conditions, for a future free from such senseless loss, was gaining momentum. Their loved ones' sacrifice would not be in vain.

*

The small and dimly lit Working Men's Club was teeming with villagers, all gathered to mourn their loved ones and pay tribute to the departed. As Elliot weaved through the crowd, he overheard bits of conversation and saw tear-stained faces. Grabbing a nearby step ladder, he climbed on top and commanded attention with a resounding clap of his hands. His heart raced, but his determination burned as he fervently urged everyone to unite, support the trust, and make a difference.

"The Trust has brought me here to take care of you fine men," he declared, his voice booming throughout the room. "I am here to advocate for better safety measures and protections for our mines and miners. As you all know too well, my heart is heavy today. Dealing with men like Charles Huntingdon is infuriating. Progress moves at a snail's pace. But I will work alongside our union leaders, parish councillors, workhouse guardians, and the Trust itself to push for real change so that tragedies like this never happen again."

"Here, here," murmured some of those standing near him, their eyes reflecting newfound determination in the face of such hardship.

Others grumbled that the official meetings had been futile and perhaps new representatives were needed to break the stalemate. The division among the men was palpable, their grief and frustration hanging heavily in the air.

"Your dedication is admirable, Elliot," said Owen, the head of the miner's union, as he offered him a firm handshake. "We have learned a painful yet valuable lesson today. Small talk with Huntingdon is getting us nowhere. A new approach is needed."

"Yes, Charles will need to spend some money to get the mine operational again. He might as well upgrade the pit at the same time."

Elliot's voice was filled with a mix of hope and frustration. Owen was amazed by the naivety of his response but chose not to enter into an angry public debate at the wake. There would be time for strategy and tough conversations in the days to come. For now, he simply nodded, his eyes filled with a feigned mix of understanding and resignation.

Under a canopy of stars, the village of Cwmgryf fell eerily silent that night as Elliot walked through its narrow streets back to his home. Shadows cast by the lamplight danced on the dark cobblestone path, mirroring the heaviness in his heart. With each step, he felt the weight of the day's events bearing down on him, the faces of the lost and the injured flashing through his mind.

"Elliot," called a weary voice from a nearby doorstep. "I heard what happened to you. I'm so sorry, but relieved you made it out alive."

It was young Tom Watts, whose face bore signs of exhaustion and illness. His eyes were sunken, his cheeks hollow, a testament to the toll the mines had taken on his body.

"Thank you, Tom," Elliot replied, offering a weak smile. "We all have our crosses to bear, don't we?"

"Indeed," the man wheezed, struggling to catch his breath. "I can't believe poor Gethin's gone. All that dust, darkness, constant fear of what might happen— it weighs on a man's soul."

"Doesn't it just," Elliot agreed, clapping a comforting hand on Tom's shoulder before continuing towards home.

The young man's words echoed in his mind, a stark reminder of the daily struggles faced by the miners of Cwmgryf.

Finally arriving home, Elliot found Ebba already in bed. Despite her exhaustion, she made an effort to smile reassuringly, her love for him shining through the weariness in her eyes.

"Come, love," she said, patting the spot next to her.

"You need rest."

"That Welsh cake looks lovely. Want to go halves?"

Elliot's voice was soft, tinged with a mix of gratitude and exhaustion.

"Of course," she said, breaking the treat neatly in half.

As they shared the snack, their weariness became undeniable. Ebba finished her last bite and yawned, snuggling deeper under the patchwork eiderdown.

Elliot stood to extinguish the oil lamp, casting the room in darkness, a darkness that now made him anxious after his ordeal. The shadows seemed to press in on him, the memory of the mine's suffocating darkness still fresh in his mind.

Just as his head touched the pillow, a loud, insistent knock echoed through the house. With a groan, Elliot threw back the blankets and made his way to the door. He pulled it open to reveal Joe, another miner, gasping for breath and clutching his chest.

CHAPTER 14

"Come in. Let me help you," Elliot said with concern, instantly recognising the signs of black lung. The man's face was ashen, his eyes wide with fear and pain.

"Thank you," Joe gasped, stumbling into the house. "I'm so s—sorry to trouble you at this late—hour—especially after the day you've had."

As Elliot guided Joe to an armchair, he glanced back at Ebba, who had risen from bed, curious and keen to assist.

"It's alright, my love. Go to bed."

Elliot knelt beside Joe, his hands firm yet gentle as he checked his pulse and listened to his laboured breathing. The miner wheezed and coughed, each desperate movement seeming to sap more of his strength.

Ebba decided to take advantage of a rare quiet moment to pen a heartfelt letter to Jess Chadwick, her adoptive mother, mother-in-law, and most importantly, lifelong confidante.

The events of the past few weeks weighed heavily on her mind, and she knew that pouring her heart out on paper would provide a much-needed release. Sat at the writing desk, the moon cast a beautiful silvery glow on the window sill. Ebba relit the oil lamp, its flickering light adding some charm to the small room. Then she picked up her fountain pen and began to write, her hand trembling a little.

Dearest Jess,

I must apologise for not writing for a few weeks now. Things have been so busy here. We hardly have a moment to ourselves. Elliot is still tirelessly advocating for improvements in the local mines, particularly at the village colliery.

My every waking moment is spent treating patients, helping deliver babies, or continuing to set up the clinic. I have very little time to rest, week in and week out. If I am honest, I find myself struggling under the weight of all that has happened here in Cwmgryf. Yesterday, we experienced a terrible tragedy—a devastating explosion in the mine claimed the lives of twenty three men. I am sure you'll read about it in the paper before this letter arrives.

Thankfully, Elliot and I are both safe, but we lost a dear friend, Gethin Williams, in the disaster.

This tragedy has left our community shattered. I cannot help but feel responsible in some way for the lives lost and the suffering that continues. We came here to help, to heal, and to protect, and we've failed.

The weight of this loss, the guilt, and the helplessness I feel— it's almost unbearable. I see the pain etched on the faces of the widows and orphans, and my heart aches for them. I can't help but question if we have truly made a difference here.

Normally, I would turn to Elliot for comfort and guidance, but this time it feels different. He's so consumed by his own grief and anger, and I fear that his unwavering focus on blaming the colliery owners might blind him to other possibilities.

I'm starting to think that diplomacy alone won't solve the deep-rooted problems plaguing our community. Perhaps a stronger stance, even a strike, is the only way to force real change. The thought terrifies me, but I can't bear to witness any more suffering.

As I write these words, my heart is heavy with sorrow and uncertainty. I long for the day when the mine will no longer pose such a threat to our community. But for now, I must face the reality of our situation and find the strength to fight for a better future.

Your loving Ebba

Ebba found solace in the act of writing. It was as if with each stroke of her pen, she was freeing herself of the heavy burden she carried. The words flowed freely, her thoughts and emotions spilling onto the page in a cathartic release. Normally, she could discuss anything with Elliot, but this time that felt inappropriate, since it felt like he was perhaps part of the problem.

Diplomacy seemed pointless in the light of recent events. Ebba felt it would be better to take a much harder stance with the colliery owner. Perhaps a short strike was the way to break the deadlock?

Everything else had seemed to prolong the agony for now. The mere thought of suggesting such a thing to Elliot filled her with trepidation, but she knew that something had to change.

It was only when she had signed the letter and tucked it away in a drawer that Ebba allowed herself a moment of proper rest. Leaning back in her writing chair, she closed her eyes and took a deep breath, imagining the day when the dangers of the mine would be a distant memory and the suffering of their community would finally ease. Even if it took a year or two, the image brought a small smile to her face, a glimmer of hope in the despair.

Alas, soon her mind raced with the usual fear and determination as she crawled back into bed alone. The soft blankets and downy pillow offered no comfort. Tomorrow would bring new challenges, ones she wasn't sure she was ready for.

But one thing was certain, the future filled her with both terror and wonderment. She could do nothing more than to wait and see what fate had in store.

CHAPTER 15

These days, the consultation room was now the village's makeshift birthing unit. Having grown fond of poor Sian, Ebba and Gwen were anxious for her upcoming difficult delivery. They couldn't wait to see her holding her precious baby, her last living reminder of husband Gethin.

Sian tried her hardest to conceal her overwhelming feeling of being left behind. She lay on the cramped examination bed, sweat cascading down her anxious face as she fought to deliver her firstborn.

"Keep pushing, Sian, you're doing marvellously," Ebba encouraged, gripping Sian's hand tightly. "It won't be much longer now."

"Aye," chimed in Gwen, gently dabbing Sian's damp brow with a fresh cloth.

Just beyond the door, Rhys Davies paced anxiously up and down the cramped hallway, his thick-soled boots clip-clopping a regular rhythm. The air was thick with the scent of sweat and blood, and his heart felt heavy with concern for his best friend's widow, left to face the world alone with a tiny bairn to care for.

He couldn't shake the nagging guilt that had settled in his chest ever since Gethin had met his untimely end in the mine collapse. How Rhys wished God had spared the much-loved married man and father-to-be, and taken a bachelor like him instead.

Sian clenched her teeth, her knuckles turning white as she gripped the bed sheets tightly. With one final, guttural cry, she pushed with all her might, and a tiny wail pierced the air. Relief washed over her like a wave, quickly followed by an overwhelming love for the tiny, squirming bundle that Gwen carefully placed into her arms.

"Congratulations, Sian, it's a lovely healthy boy," announced Gwen, her eyes shining with pride. "And he's the spit of your Gethin."

"Thank you both so much," Sian managed to whisper through her tears, her voice shaking from exhaustion, emotion and relief they had both survived the birth.

*

The feeling of relief was short-lived as Sian realised the harsh reality of being a mining widow. She struggled to make ends meet for her newborn son in their small, drafty cottage. Basic necessities like food and heating were now unaffordable luxuries. She didn't want to seem ungrateful, but the kind neighbours meagre help wasn't enough.

With over two dozen men killed at once, the Trust's funds were quickly depleting, and further payments were delayed while a plan was developed to sustain it.

Discussions were had and cuts were made to the payments. Now they barely covered the rent and nothing else. Desperation clawed at her heart and hunger pangs plagued her belly. Working at the shop with a child was stressful. Sometimes she felt so exhausted and overwhelmed with being a new mother that she was simply unable to work a full shift.

Feeling a pit in her stomach, she scanned the village for any solutions. Her gaze landed on the delivery men who came through weekly with supplies from the train station. A desperate idea crept into her mind but she quickly pushed it away, although it refused to stay there.

As the days passed and her hunger worsened, the thought of sleeping with a stranger for just ten minutes to earn enough money for food for her and her baby became more tempting. She could feel her morals slipping away as she considered this unthinkable option, but it seemed like the least unpleasant choice among all her other hardships.

The many travelling delivery men would surely suffice. It didn't have to be a local man. The idea of being intimate with someone she knew and facing the resulting gossip felt like a step too far. And so, with a heavy heart, she began to seriously contemplate this dangerous path to survive.

She cradled baby Gethin in her arms, rocking him gently as she stared into the flickering flames of the meagre fire in the Working Men's Club. Could she really subject herself to such a life?

But what other option did she have?

As her son stirred, his tiny fists flailing in the air, Sian made a silent vow. She would do whatever it took to ensure his survival, even if it meant sacrificing her own dignity and pride. The thought terrified her, but she steeled herself and whispered a promise into the chilly night air as she trudged home alone.

"Whatever it takes, my darling, I'll do it for you."

CHAPTER 16

As the sun began to set, a soft and almost hesitant knock sounded at Sian's door. Rhys stood in the doorway, his face smudged with coal dust, his clothes caked with dirt. His eyes widened as they took in the sight of Sian's gaunt face, her once-rosy cheeks now hollowed out from a lack of food. In her arms, she held her baby tightly, swaddled in threadbare clothes that barely protected the bairn against the cold.

"Rhys, what brings you here?"

"Can't I come to see how you're faring?" Rhys replied gruffly, trying to mask his concern.

He glanced down at the baby, who stirred and whimpered softly as he wriggled his face free from the folds of his blanket. He stared the visitor directly in the eye. Guilt wracked Rhys; it felt like his best friend Gethin was staring back at him, reminding him it was his duty to do more for his widow.

"How's the little one?"

"Struggling," Sian admitted, her voice cracking as she sobbed. "I don't mean to complain, but with Gethin gone, it's been hard to make ends meet. And I am so afraid, Rhys. What's going to happen to us? I've not eaten for days. What if my milk stops? And that brute Gerald Price has been demanding the rent. Menacing, he was."

As she broke down into inconsolable tears and sank down on her rickety bed, the metal frame groaning, Rhys sat alongside and put his comforting arm around her shoulder.

"Look, Sian," Rhys said, his voice heavy with emotion. "I'll talk to my father. I am sure you can lodge with us for the time being. That will save you a bit of money. I won't see you suffer like this, or be bullied by that ogre of a foreman."

Sian looked up at him, her eyes red with tears. She wanted to agree to his kind offer, but didn't want to relinquish the privacy her one-room cottage afforded her.

As if on cue, Ebba appeared at the door, her crisp white apron standing out against the grime of the village.

"Hello Sian, I am just doing my rounds. Come, let me check the baby," Ebba said gently, easing the infant from Rhys's arms.

As she examined the tiny child, Rhys paced the room.

"Ebba," he began hesitantly, "do you think there might be any posts available with the Trust? Sian can't stay here on her own like this?"

"Rhys, I'll do my best to find out," Ebba promised. "But things are all a bit chaotic at the moment."

She was interrupted by a wail from the distressed baby. Rhys looked troubled. While he was sure his father would take in Sian, a wailing baby in the same room was another matter entirely. Owen was already exhausted from tramping the neighbouring valleys for day labouring work. He needed his sleep to keep working so hard.

Ebba looked at him sympathetically, understanding his frustration that he couldn't do more.

> "I know it's difficult, Sian. But we'll all pitch in where we can. We'll find a way, one step at a time."

When her visitors left, with the baby asleep in her arms, Sian pulled the curtain to one side, making a mental note as she eyed the movements of the night-shift delivery men.

True to their word, Rhys and Ebba managed to secure a temporary home for Sian at the village shop. Mrs Morgan, the shopkeeper, agreed to take her in, knowing how desperate she was. Now her shop work could cover her food outlay. Alas, no one predicted this arrangement would add fuel to the simmering tension between the widow and Mr Price.

Behind closed doors, Gerald Price had a formidable reputation for abusing his authority as the unruly enforcer in the village. He was furious that his chance to take advantage of beautiful Sian was now gone.

> "Are you sure I won't be a burden, Mrs Morgan?" Sian asked hesitantly, pressing a gentle kiss to Gethin's downy head, relieved that he had finally settled after a long, fussy spell.

"Oh lass, we all need a helping hand every now and then," Mrs Morgan replied with a gentle smile. "You've been an excellent employee for years, as you well know. So please, don't fret—it's fine."

Later that evening, Rhys helped her move her few keepsakes to the shop, then excused himself. He stomped off, a smug grin on his face as he headed to the post office to gleefully inform the foreman in writing that the Williams' cottage was now vacant. The implication was clear: any chance of the foreman exploiting Sian's vulnerable position was gone.

Sian was grateful for the older woman's generosity. Finally, it seemed things were easing up a little for her. As she settled into her new temporary home in a small room at the back, she prayed that Rhys's actions with Gerald wouldn't bring more hardship upon them all. How a man so cruel could be distantly related to someone as caring as Gwen was an eternal mystery to the village folk.

The early morning sun peeked through the grimy windows of the village shop. Sian shivered as she reached for another consignment of tinned corned beef to stack on the shelves, her fingers numb from the cold. She tried to concentrate on her work, but her mind kept drifting back to the foreman and his menacing behaviour. Eventually, the monotony of the repetitive manual work sent her into a trance.

The trance was broken as the shop door jangled open, letting in a gust of cold wind and Gerald Price.

"Good day, Mrs Morgan," he said with a sneer, his eyes scanning over Sian. "I heard you took in a stray."

"Mr Price, always a pleasure," Mrs Morgan replied, her voice strained. "Sian is not a stray, she has been an excellent worker for years as you well know. So, what can I do for you?"

"Actually, I need to speak with young Sian here," Gerald said, his voice oozing malice. "In private. Some business with the cottage."

"Very well." Mrs Morgan hesitated before disappearing into the storeroom, leaving Sian alone with the beast.

"Listen here, girl," he growled, cornering her against the shelves. "Davies may have gotten you this roof over your head, but don't think it means you're safe from me."

"Please," Sian whispered, tears welling in her eyes as Gerald's hands roamed over her. "Don't."

"Know your place, girl," he hissed, his breath hot on her face. "And understand that your precious Rhys can't protect you from everything."

Gerald left her trembling amidst the jars and tins, his cruel laughter ringing in her ears. Sian fought to regain her composure, but fear gripped her throat, suffocating her.

"Is everything alright?" Mrs Morgan asked when she returned, concern etched on her face.

"I'm fine," Sian managed through clenched teeth, avoiding eye contact. "He thinks I am in arrears, but I'm not."

Unable to bear it any longer, Sian sought comfort in Ebba's company and poured out the dark thoughts that haunted her since losing Gethin. Ebba listened attentively, her eyes filled with quiet strength.

"Remember, you're not alone. We'll get through this together. Rhys and Owen can have a word with Gerald and put him in his place."

And as Sian allowed herself to be enveloped in the warm embrace of friendship, she felt a flicker of hope ignite within her heart.

Ebba and Elliot were troubled by Sian's story. They agreed that something needed to be done about Gerald Price, but they didn't want to put Sian in danger.

"Elliot, can you walk these two home please?"

"Of course, m'lady! Whatever you want! Sian, are you ready?" he said with a playful bow.

"Yes! Come on. Stop making a fuss!"

Later, as Sian settled in for the night, dozing on a cold straw mattress next to her newborn 's plush little basket, she couldn't shake off the day's events. Despite Ebba and Elliot's assurance that they would help deal with Price, she still felt a sense of unease at the thought of him. She had always known he was a cruel and ruthless man, but today he had crossed a line by threatening her directly.

As she closed her eyes and tried to drift off into sleep, she heard a noise coming from the back door of the shop. Her senses were heightened as she recognised the sound of a key slipping into the lock.

Her heart raced as she pretended to be asleep while keeping an eye on the intruder through barely open eyes.

Gerald Price tiptoed towards her sleeping form, his silhouette looming over her. He stopped at the edge of her mattress and leaned down towards her face, his calloused hand covering her mouth before she could make any noise.

CHAPTER 17

"Not a sound!" he hissed, malice shimmering in his eyes as he forced her onto her back, crushing the air out of her.

The clanging of his belt buckle echoed in Sian's ears, filling her with a deep sense of dread. She did everything she could to block out the pain and humiliation of the brutal assault that followed, praying for it to end quickly. But for the young widow, time seemed to stand still as she endured every agonising minute at the mercy of this monstrous man.

"You'll keep doing this, or I'll tell Mrs Morgan you've been nicking her stock," he said to Sian's motionless form. He strutted over and swiped a tin of corned beef from the shelf and shoved, tucking it into his pocket with a smirk.

"You agree to keep our little secret? Do ya? Answer me!—"

"—Yes," mumbled a tearful Sian.

"I'm glad we understand each other. Be a good lass tomorrow and I might put this tin back," Price warned, as he gently shut the back door behind him.

Sian endured the same for three nights before Mrs

Morgan sensed her disheartenment but not the reason for it, the lass having fibbed.

> "If you're feeling off, go see Ebba," the shopkeeper suggested. "Hurry now, you'll be back in a jiffy. I'll keep an eye on Baby Gethin while you're gone."

*

Price's narrowed eyes watched Sian's hunched figure scurry across the green, her arms wrapped tightly around herself. Her steps were quick and unsteady, as if she were trying to escape an invisible foe.

Upon arrival, Sian burst into tears, and it didn't take long for Ebba to figure out what was really going on. Enraged, the young doctor swore to put an end to Price's mistreatment once and for all.

> "And don't worry about finding a place to stay. The storeroom may be cramped but it's secure."

As the siren blared, signalling the end of another day at the colliery, the Chadwicks headed over to Rhys and Owen's house.

> "This is unforgivable," Rhys muttered through clenched fists. "Gerald Price will not get away with what he has done to these women."

> "We must proceed with caution," Elliot warned. "We need solid evidence against him and we don't want to provoke any retaliation."

"He's right," Ebba chimed in. "We need support from other women who have been hurt by him or know someone who has. It won't be easy, but he needs to face consequences for his actions."

"I know," Rhys said, determination in his eyes. "

"Could you ask Gwen to speak to the other women? They trust her. We need to put a stop to it."

Later that day, at the local Working Men's club, whispers of retribution grew louder. Angry voices demanded justice for Gerald's victims and called for an end to his reign of terror.

"We want him fired and banished from the village, don't we, lads?" Owen barked, which was met with a cheer.

However, as Huntingdon's right-hand man, removing him would not be an easy feat. Yet, as the people of Cwmgryf united in their quest for justice, the air crackled with a newfound sense of purpose —a collective resolve to expose Gerald Price's villainy and finally protect the vulnerable from his grasp.

When rumours of trouble ahead reached Gerald Price's ears, a malicious smile stretched across his face as he made his way towards Mrs Morgan's shop. He clutched the stolen tin of corned beef tightly in his fingers, relishing in the satisfaction it would bring him.

With each step closer to the shop, the words sharpened in his mind. They would pierce through the illusion of Sian's innocence, exposing the rot beneath. He would lay bare her pilfering. He would suggest Mrs Morgan demand justice, retribution for the young woman's crimes against decency and trust.

The possibility of witnessing Sian's downfall before his own brought him joy, and he eagerly anticipated making it a reality.

He might be on the verge of losing everything, but one thing was certain: he wouldn't go down without a fight.

CHAPTER 18

Charles Huntingdon stood by the window of his drawing-room, his eagle eyes twitching as he watched the group of officials enter his colliery's main entrance.

The surprise reopening inspection had rendered him livid, and he clenched his fists so tightly he felt his Freemason's ring dig into his stubby fingers. He knew he'd cut corners with the mine's refurbishment to maintain profits, planning to make further improvements once the colliery was operational again. He never imagined he'd be subjected to a full inspection so soon. Despite the mine being closed and no wages to pay, his fixed costs continued to pile up at an alarming rate.

"Damn them," he cursed, his breathing heavy with anger.

Six hours later, the inspectors called a meeting to present their findings before producing their official report. In the boardroom, Huntingdon straightened his tie and mentally prepared himself for what he anticipated would be a stormy encounter.

"Let them in now, would you, Gerald."

The oak-panelled room was tense, the chairs filled by the six inspectors, plus Reverend Jenkins, Elliot, Owen and Rhys Davies. Henry Blackwood flanked the colliery owner. As the inspectors presented their main findings, Charles's anger grew with each word spoken.

Lead investigator, Mr Cox, cleared his throat and opened the meeting:

> "After inspecting the Cwmgryf Colliery following the explosion, I have serious concerns about safety.
>
> Firstly, the ventilation system is not up to scratch. Despite supposed repairs, I still found pockets of firedamp—er, methane gas—in multiple areas. Airflow remains poor and air quality questionable, indicating inadequate fans and/or air shafts. My recommendation: double the air shafts and upgrade all fans.
>
> Furthermore, I saw coal dust suspended in the air throughout lower levels of the mine even though production has stopped. We all know how explosive this dust can be, as evidenced by the secondary explosions during the recent disaster.
>
> Clearly, dust suppression measures are failing. My previous recommendation applies here too.
>
> The mine's structural integrity is also compromised. I noticed numerous cracks in the wooden supports already, patches of unstable rock overhead, and other signs that the probability of roof falls remains high. Recommendation: All degraded sections of rock

liable to collapse are to be removed, and all wooden supports not fixed during the recent repairs are to be replaced.

Furthermore, an examination of the equipment revealed a small quantity of open-flame lamps. The mine management must ensure that only approved safety lamps are used and that they are properly maintained. The recent disaster damaged or depleted much of the rescue equipment.

In terms of readiness, the mine is lacking. The escape routes are poorly marked, communication systems are unreliable. In the event of another accident, I fear that the miners would be ill-equipped to escape or receive timely assistance.

The record-keeping at the colliery is also below the required standard. Some essential records were not made or I suspect have been withheld from my inspectors. I struggled to find accurate records of structural inspections, repairs, and safety checks, raising doubts about the mine's previous compliance with regulations.

Onto the good news— "

Charles' face remained thunderous.

"The buildings and working practices above ground are reasonable and not a cause for concern. What's more, the work and overtime rotas indicate that working hour limits were not being breached prior to the accident, but I am afraid, Mr Huntingdon, those are the only pieces of good news.

In conclusion, Cwmgryf Colliery is not in a fit state to reopen. I need not remind you that the men who work in this mine and their families deserve swift action and effective changes.

Once the necessary adjustments have been made, another inspection will be required. Only then can I ensure the safety of this facility."

The costs for meeting these requests would be astronomical, enough to jeopardise the Huntingdon's entire family legacy, let alone impinge on his current lifestyle.

"Outrageous!" Charles barked, slamming his fist on the table. "This will cost a small fortune! I'd rather close the mine than bankrupt myself over this nonsense!"

"As you wish. The full report will be with you within seven days. Gentlemen, our work here is done. Good day to you, Mr Huntingdon."

Alone now, Charles paced his luxurious boardroom, the inspector's words ringing in his ears. His mind raced, trying to calculate the expense of the additional safety measures. It would cut into his profits, force him to sell off some of his prized possessions. The mere thought made his stomach churn. He had worked tirelessly to build this empire, to secure his family's legacy, and now it seemed to be slipping away.

But as he paused by the window, gazing out at the smoggy village that owed its existence to him, a flicker of doubt sparked within him. He thought of the miner's faces, all their lives intertwined with the fate of the colliery and the uneasy body between them. Could he really sacrifice their well-being for his own ambition?

A war raged inside him—the selfish desire to protect his wealth and status against the growing realisation of the human cost. And as the shadows grew longer, a fragile determination began to bloom.

He would find a way to make the mine safe, to protect the men who had served him so faithfully. It wouldn't be easy or cheap, but as his wife Elizabeth would tell him later over dinner, it was the only path that would allow him to face himself in the mirror each day.

Later, the Working Men's Club filled with the murmur of worried voices as the miners' leaders gathered to discuss the implications of the inspection.

> "We can't let this happen again," Tom Watts said. "My poor brother's life was worth more than any lump of coal."

Heads nodded in agreement, but a worried whisper rippled through the crowd.

"What about our jobs? Feeding our families? We need to get back to work—and quickly"

"Safety comes first. Nothing else matters if we're not alive to provide for our loved ones."

The debate raged on, a tangle of desperation and defiance. But as the night wore on, a grudging consensus emerged. They would work with Huntingdon, not against him.

"So, we're agreed, men?" said Owen Davies. "We will push to help make the mine safe, for us, for our fallen brothers, and for the future of their village. Let's take a vote—those in favour raise your hand."

The 'ayes' had it. It was a gamble, but it was the only chance they had.

Through the windows of the club, a few men caught sight of Huntingdon's carriage as it made its way towards his country estate. Pints of ale sloshed on the table as the glasses were quickly set down. The sound of hobnail boots echoed in the lane outside.

With great courage, the men stepped in front of the muscular brown horse. The carriage slowed to a halt, and Huntingdon peered out the window, his face pale. Owen stepped forward, his voice ringing clear in the chilly evening air.

"Mr Huntingdon, we have a proposition for you."

A tense silence hung in the air, broken only by the snorting of the horse. In that moment, the future of the mine, and perhaps the entire village, hung in the balance.

CHAPTER 19

"Mr Huntingdon, we've discussed it and we're willing to help with the repairs," said Owen as his employer's eyes widened in surprise.

"You will?"

"Yes," Owen confirmed, "we'll provide our labour for free as long as you cover the cost of materials. And until the work is completed, we ask that our rent be waived."

A moment of calculation passed over Huntingdon's as a tight-lipped smile forming on his dry lips.

"Thank you. It's settled then. Mr Price will meet you at the colliery gates tomorrow morning to discuss plans and get started. Good day to you."

As the miners retreated like a dark tide, the carriage of Charles Huntingdon made its way home once more, the crack of the whip serving as a menacing warning in the stillness of the night. The steady beat of hooves on cobblestone gave way to an eerie silence as the glossy black carriage melted into the darkness.

*

Later that evening, engineer Henry Blackwood went for a stroll to clear his mind, only to run into Elliot on his way back from a house visit.

"I have a confession, Elliot. It was me who reported Charles' plans to reopen the mine to the inspectors. I couldn't bear to see those men put their lives at risk again in such dire conditions. The deaths of twenty three innocent souls have weighed heavily on my conscience. Of course, Charles is unaware of my involvement."

"I see."

"I've decided to retire and wash my hands of that place forever. Perhaps it will remain closed until it's properly fixed. But knowing Charles, he'll likely take the easy route and try to sell it for profit. But until someone buys it and is prepared to invest in its future, he'll be stuck with a money pit instead of a working pit—and all those poor men will be out of work. The village is now so bitterly divided. Some men value greater safety. Others are willing to take risks. I fear that my actions have led to more suffering than I hoped to prevent"

Dr Blackwood shook his head, his hands clasped tightly together.

"Haven't you heard, Henry? A band of the men plan to volunteer to fix the mine's issues? Production will begin in days, if Charles can secure the materials they need."

However, the news didn't reach the faces of the two men, who still looked gravely concerned.

"But who will take your place, Henry? Who will ensure the welfare of these men? Certainly not Mr Price."

"That's a question I cannot answer," Blackwood whispered, his shoulders slumped in defeat. "I can only hope that another engineer with the same dedication to the miners' welfare will come forward as I had tried to do—under very trying circumstances."

*

The night air was bitterly cold, and the wind seemed to howl Cwmgryf's name. The rumour of Dr Blackwood's retirement spread like wildfire through the village, causing a tense unease among the villagers. They gathered in small groups, huddled close together as they discussed their fears and concerns about being left at the mercy of Charles Huntington's penny-pinching ways.

Bryn, the town troublemaker, stood at the head of one group. His wild hair and unshaven face added to his menacing appearance as he stirred up anger and resentment towards the Chadwicks.

"I bet those doctors were the ones who tipped off the inspectors," he growled. "Them outsiders don't care about us hard-working miners. They just want to get their name in the paper for being righteous. Meddlers both of 'em."

Whispers and nods of agreement rippled through the group.

"Bryn's always had it in for the Chadwicks, ain't he," one miner said to another.

"But we can't deny there might be some truth to what he's saying," the other admitted reluctantly.

"They may have helped your daughter when she fell ill, but that doesn't change the fact that they're not one of us."

"We need to find answers," Bryn declared, his voice filled with malice, "—and I'm more than willing to extract them from those two. "

*

Sat in Uncle Ifan's small front room, the postman delivered a note for Gwen. Things weren't terribly rosy for her either.

My dearest darling Gwen,

I pray that this letter finds you in good health during these difficult times. I have been reflecting deeply on our current situation. My heart is burdened with sorrow. How I wish to see you, to talk this over in person, but with my ship docked in

Liverpool for some time yet, the written word must be enough.

The thought of the mine closing permanently fills me with dread, not only for the loss of our jobs but also for the impact it would have on our community. Cwmgryf has been our home for many years and holds a special place in our hearts.

Our wedding day is something we both eagerly anticipate, but given the uncertainty surrounding the mine's future and our jobs, I fear we may have no choice but to postpone—at least for now.

I am not suggesting we delay our wedding indefinitely, but rather wait until we have a clearer understanding of what lies ahead for the colliery. I understand how difficult this decision is, but I feel it is a wise one.

How can we set up our home and start a family, if it were to fall to pieces soon after?

Please know that my love for you remains unshakable, and my longing to make you my wife is as strong as ever.

Yours,

Llewelyn

*

Meanwhile, at the small clinic, now overflowing with injured miners from the blast, the young couple had sought counsel from Elliot's parents. When it became clear they were being blamed for the inspection they had written to John and Jess. A plump envelope had arrived with a response, which they ripped open.

Dear Elliot and Ebba,

After the terrible disaster we were so relieved to receive your latest letter and we hope that this message finds you well, despite the trying circumstances you currently face.

We are deeply troubled to hear about the accusations against you about instigating the inspection.

During our time running our Salvation Army citadel, we often found ourselves caught in conflicts. The key is to maintain your neutrality.

Don't allow yourselves to be pulled into the chaos. Your role is to heal, comfort, and support those who rely on your expertise and kindness, not enter into angry discussions.

Your work in Cwmgryf exemplifies the values of organisations like the Tredegar Medical Aid Society, which has also provided vital assistance to the working class community in South Wales. You are paving the way for a future, where access to healthcare is a right for the working class, not a privilege. People will soon change their opinions of you as you continue with your reforms.

Remember, you are not alone in this struggle. The Salvation Army and Miner's Benevolent Trust both believe in your project. Your efforts are making a significant difference. Amidst the growing divide within the village, let your clinic stand as a symbol of hope and unity. Show the people of Cwmgryf that they all deserve compassion, respect, and dignity.

Our thoughts and prayers are with you and everyone in the village. May you find the strength, wisdom, and resilience to overcome this challenge.

With heartfelt affection,

Your mother and father.

As nightfall descended upon the village, Gwen and Llewellyn faced the heartache of postponing their nuptials, while Elliot resolved to remain steadfast in their mission to serve the people, and Ebba focused on helping the vulnerable women.

Little did they know that all their courage and dedication would soon be tested like never before, as the shadows of uncertainty grew ever darker on the horizon.

Ebba's face remained downcast as she observed the main hall at the humble Working Men's Club, noting the worried expressions on the faces of the miners' wives and widows, seated on the well-worn wooden benches.

The rain pattered against the windows as she took to the small raised stage.

"Ladies. Thank you all for coming at this late hour," she began, her voice steady. "I've called this meeting to discuss the widows' fund, which I'm sure you're all aware has been dwindling due to the uncertainty surrounding the mine's future, and the number of women needing assistance."

A murmur of agreement swept through the room.

"We must come together and forge a path forward. Many of you face the grim prospect of the workhouse if we cannot find a solution. But we will find a solution."

One woman, her eyes red and swollen from recent tears, raised her hand hesitantly.

"But what can we do, Dr Chadwick? Yes, many of the men are volunteering to fix the mine, but what if that's not enough? What if Huntingdon decides he wants to be rid of the place and closes it."

"As always, we will support each other. We may not have all the answers, but together we can find a way. My husband is collaborating with the Trust and neighbouring miner's unions to explore options. We have also applied for a government hardship grant. Our situation is dire, but not hopeless. And there is still the hope that the volunteers making the repairs will keep Mr Huntingdon from making a snap decision to walk away."

*

If only they had known how slowly the mine repairs would creep along, despite everyone's attempts to stay optimistic.

The agonising days dragged on as the situation in the village seemed to worsen with each passing hour. As the last of their savings evaporated, many widows, terrified by the prospect of Gerald Price's predatory demands, abandoned their homes and sought refuge with relatives in neighbouring villages. The once-tight knit community began to unravel under the weight of fear and uncertainty. Those who remained clung to the fading hope that the mine would reopen soon and life would return to normal.

*

The air inside the clubhouse was thick with tension as miners and their families gathered together all the information they had, desperate to glean something accurate about the mine's future. Ebba could feel the anxiety vibrating through the room, and she shared in the villagers' mounting unease.

"Have you heard anything?" asked Elliot, nursing his pint while scanning the faces around him for a glimmer of hope.

"I wish I had something to tell you," Owen replied, pushing his beer mat around the table in frustration. "But we're just as much in the dark as you are. Without Blackwood to help us comply with the legislation, all we can do is try our best."

The ticking of the club's grandfather clock seemed to grow louder with each passing second, as if counting down to another impending disaster that, this time, would consume them all.

Bryn Jones muttered about the impossible situation they were in. The volunteers worked tirelessly while others did nothing. Widows were the priority, but what about the men? They had a roof over their heads, but not enough food thanks to dwindling savings.

Ebba exchanged a worried glance with Elliot, as she caught snippets of conversations around her. It was clear that the divisions within the community were growing more pronounced by the day, and she feared for what might happen if they couldn't find a way to heal the rifts.

Suddenly a hush fell over the room as the door creaked open, revealing the imposing figure of Charles Huntingdon, tipped off by his enforcer, Gerald Price. All eyes turned to the colliery owner, who strode in with a grim expression.

"Listen up, men!" he barked, silencing the last whispers of conversation. "I've had enough of dithering and delays. Tomorrow, I'll be making an important announcement concerning the future of the mine. Be there at the colliery gates—nine o'clock sharp."

A collective gasp rippled through the hall, as villagers exchanged anxious glances, their hearts heavy with dread.

"What will become of all of us?" whispered Ebba, her voice laden with fear as she clung to her open-mouthed husband.

CHAPTER 20

The church bells rang out nine loud chimes. A hush fell over the crowd at the sight of Charles Huntington negotiating the steps to a makeshift podium. He surveyed them with a steely gaze, his fine suit a stark contrast to their worn and patched clothing.

> "I will not be closing or selling the mine." Huntington declared, his voice booming across the yard, accompanied by a relieved sigh then excited murmurs.

The colliery owner raised a hand for silence.

> "However, we must speed up the pace and quality of the repairs. Thus, I have arranged for a group of experienced miners and engineers from my Llanwryl colliery to manage the structural refurbishment effort. They will work alongside you, especially those already familiar with the nuances of our mine's layout."

The initial relief that had washed over the villagers began to dissipate as they exchanged uncertain glances. Old Huw, leaning heavily on his cane, spoke up.

> "Are you paying these outsiders to come here? Our lads have not earned tuppence since the blast."

Huntington fixed him with a cold stare.

"The task force's expertise is essential. They will oversee the critical work to bring the mine back to full capacity. That remains my priority."

"What about our wages?" called out another voice from the crowd. "Will we be fairly compensated?"

Huntington's eyes narrowed.

"As we've discussed, once the mine is up and running, you'll be fairly compensated for your hard work. However, I must warn against making unrealistic demands. The survival of this mine rests in all of our hands. As you know, with the influx of cheap imports, coal prices have plummeted and mines are barely scraping by. Rest assured, my expectations of Cwmgryfs' workers are not excessive. We must work together if we want to succeed."

The villagers dispersed, their earlier excitement dampened by unease. Rhys Davies watched as Huntington descended from the podium. The younger miner's jaw clenched, his thoughts racing.

"He speaks of fairness," Rhys muttered to his father, "but I fear it's just another empty promise. These outsiders will only look down on us and leave us with the most dangerous and dirty work, while they sit back and collect their wages from Llanwryl. Huntingdon always takes us for fools!"

Owen placed a reassuring hand on his son's shoulder.

"We must be patient, Rhys. The reopening of the mine is a blessing, no matter how it comes about. But we must stay vigilant. We cannot let these new arrivals push us aside."

As they made their way back to their cottage, Rhys couldn't shake the feeling that Huntington's announcement was just the beginning of a fresh series of challenges for the villager's.

*

Within two hours of the announcement, the village was transformed. Residents looked on as a thunderous convoy of at least twenty carts, each flatbed piled high with equipment and supplies, rumbled into the village. Atop each cart perched an army of men, their minds and flesh hardened by years of toil in neighbouring Llanwryl. The shire horses strained against their harnesses, their flanks heaving as they hauled the heavy loads through the swirling dust.

As the carts drew closer, just inside the colliery gates, Rhys could make out the figure of a mountain of a man seated in the first truck's passenger seat. Even at a distance, the newcomer's bearing exuded authority, his posture ramrod straight and his gaze fixed resolutely ahead.

"That must be the foreman Huntington mentioned," Owen remarked, wiping his brow with the back of his hand. "Looks like a right taskmaster, he does."

Rhys nodded, watching as the trucks rolled to a stop near the mine entrance. The foreman, broad-shouldered, with close-cropped greying hair, jumped down from the cab, and barked orders to the men who leapt down in unison from the other carts.

"Alright, lads, let's get this equipment unloaded and set up," the foreman called out, his voice carrying across the cluttered yard. "We've got a tight schedule to keep, and I won't have any lollygagging on my watch."

As the work crew set about their tasks, Rhys and Owen approached, eager to size up the new arrivals. The foreman, noticing their approach, turned to face them, his steely blue eyes appraising the pair.

"Jack Thompson," he said by way of introduction, extending a calloused hand. "I'll be overseeing the repairs and making sure this mine is up to snuff."

Owen shook the proffered hand, his grip firm.

"Owen Davies, and this is my son, Rhys. We're local miners, born and bred."

Thompson gave a curt nod.

"Excellent. You'll be working under my team's supervision, lads. We've got engineers and surveyors to assess the damages and plan the repairs. Your job will be to clear the rubble, haul materials, and lend a hand with the rebuilding. It'll be hard work, but if we all pull together, we'll have this mine ready for inspection in no time."

Union man Rhys bristled at the implication that the local miners were seen as mere manual labourers, but he held his tongue. He knew that cooperation was key for the success of the repairs, no matter how begrudgingly given.

As Thompson turned back to his team, Rhys caught sight of a familiar figure making his way across the green, his black cassock billowing in the breeze.

> "Gentlemen! Reverend Jenkins of St David's. I trust you are looking forward to settling in? I just wanted to offer my services, should any of you need religious guidance during your time here."

Thompson looked down his long nose at the man.

> "I appreciate the offer, Reverend, but we're here to work, not pray."

> "Of course, of course. But do remember, Mr Thompson, that faith can be a powerful tool in times of adversity."

With a sigh, Rhys and Owen strode towards the mine entrance, steeling' themselves for the hard work ahead. The fate of Cwmgryf hung in the balance, and they knew that every man, whether local or outsider, would have to give his all to secure a future for the village and its people.

The deadline was only days away, and if the mine failed the inspection, this time, there would be only one outcome: closure.

CHAPTER 21

Sweat poured down Owen's brow as he hefted another wooden beam into place, his muscles straining with the effort. Around him, the other miners toiled in the dim light, their faces streaked with grime and exhaustion. Most of the Llanwryl members stood nearby alongside Jack Thompson, poring over blueprints and discussing the next phase of the repairs.

> "Oi, Thompson!" Owen called out, his voice ragged with fatigue. "When are you lot going to get your hands dirty? We've been at this for hours while you stand around chatting like gossiping washerwomen."

Jack Thompson looked up from his plans, his eyes narrowing.

> "Watch your tongue, sir. We're here to make sure this mine is safe and functional, not to do your job for you."

> "Do our job?" Rhys interjected, stepping forward. "We're the ones risking our necks down here, clearing the debris and shoring up the walls. What have you lot done besides stare at plans?"

The other Cwmgryf miners murmured in agreement, their frustration palpable. Thompson opened his mouth to retort, but before he could speak, Tom Watt's voice cut through the tension.

"Gentlemen, please! We're all working towards the same goal here. Fighting amongst ourselves will only make the task harder—and slower, the last thing we need!"

"If everyone put their back into it, we'd be done quicker and spend less time breathing in coal dust and risking cave-ins every minute," Owen scoffed.

Thompson cleared his throat, looking chastened.

"Whatever differences we may have, we're all here for the same reason: to reopen this colliery. Let's just get the job done within seven days. No more bleating; more grafting. Save your debating for the Working Men's Club in your own time. I am not here to be liked. I am here to rebuild this pit. Now, are you with me or not?"

Labour relations did not improve over the coming days, but at least the condition of the mine did.

Jack Thompson might have been the most unpopular man above and below ground in the mine, but he was certainly Huntingdon's most effective foreman by far.

*

Inspection day quickly arrived, heavy with tension and anxiety. Everyone understood the high stakes at play if the mine failed to pass government inspection. The clinic was buzzing with talk of what would happen.

"It's time," Elliot uttered, his voice thick with emotion. "The men have given their all. Now we must trust in their hard work."

"I just hope it's enough," his wife whispered.

The hours dragged on, each minute feeling like an eternity as they waited for news from the mine. Ebba paced around the clinic, trying to imagine what an inspection entailed. She had heard chatter from the men, but never having been inside a mine, it was difficult to envision.

As Elliot's pocket watch showed noon, a figure emerged from the mine on the other side of town. It was Jack Thompson, out of breath from running up to the entrance—grinning from ear to ear.

"We did it!" he shouted, his voice echoing across the yard. "Passed with flying colours!"

A cheer went up from the gathered crowd, the tension of the day releasing in a wave of relief and joy. Some miners embraced their families as they celebrated the miraculous victory. Others ran to tell their loved ones.

As Tom Watts burst through the main door of the clinic with the news, Ebba felt her own eyes well up. They had done it. Against all odds. The people of Cwmgryf had come together and saved their mine.

Elliot moved closer and stole a kiss from his loving wife, causing a loud cheer from their patients.

Amidst the jubilation and revelry, Rhys couldn't shake the persistent unease that their hardships were far from resolved. Despite their hard-earned triumph, he could still feel the deep wounds of past injustices. Though bandaged, they remained raw and festering beneath the surface. Huntington's stubborn refusal to even acknowledge their union felt like a never-ending slap in the face.

The fiery young activist paced, his fists clenched tightly in his pockets as he surveyed the jubilant scene before him. But amidst the joy, the shrewd campaigner sensed the same grievances would still linger, waiting for the right moment to boil over and reignite the feuding once again.

As Ebba watched the miners celebrate, she caught sight of Rhys slipping away from the crowd towards the Working Men's Club, his face a mask of determination. She knew where he was going, and her heart ached for the battle he was about to wage.

But for now, she, like the others, would savour this moment of triumph.

*

"It's not right, I tell you," grumbled Owen Davies, clutching his pint. "We've slaved away getting that mine repaired in record time—days not weeks—risking our lives, and for what? No wage and no say in how things are run in future."

Murmurs of agreement rippled through the club hall, the men nodding their heads in solidarity.

> "And what about our safety? Old Huntingdon never does more than the bare minimum." chimed in another grizzly miner, his eyes blazing with anger.

> "I agree," added Rhys. "There's one more measly ventilation shaft and a few new lamps, but not much else apart from more struts and less fallen rubble! Those fancy inspectors and engineers, they don't know the first thing about what it's like working down there, day in and out. All those near misses. It's a wonder we're not all dead, let alone the twenty three men cruelly taken. It's us, always us who bear the brunt of the danger, not the powers that be at the colliery."

As the dissatisfaction crept back over the next few days, Rhys was certain that the only way to improve the lives of the miners and their loved ones was through united effort. However, after reading about the brutal Featherstone massacre in the paper, where armed forces shot at protesting miners and innocent men lost their lives on Yorkshire's moors, he couldn't stress enough how important it was for them to act shrewdly.

The desperation on the faces of his fellow miners and their starving children fuelled Rhys's determination. Calling for a strike was a risky move, but it was one they had to make. He couldn't sit idly by and watch his comrades suffer any longer. Doing nothing would only prolong the pain for everyone involved.

Not wanting to do anything hasty, he decided to see Sian at the clinic. He knocked gently on the door and when she opened it, her face lit up with a smile that took his breath away.

> "Rhys, what brings you here?" she asked, ushering him inside. "Why aren't you celebrating with the others?"

He took a deep breath, searching her eyes for the courage he needed.

> "Sian, I'm worried about what's to come. While I am grateful that the colliery is opening again, Huntingdon knows we worked for free. I can see that toad cutting our wages and expecting us to roll over like puppies having their bellies rubbed—you mark my words! Huntingdon is greedy. Always out for himself, he is. Plain and simple. I was going to talk to my da about it tonight."

Sian reached out and took his hand, her touch sending a tingle through his body and her words filled him with a sense of purpose.

> "You're the real leader, Rhys, not Owen, whether you realise it or not. The men look up to you, and they trust you to fight for what's right. Your Da's older than you, not as hungry ."

"Sian, I don't know if I'm ready for this, but I feel compelled to try. For our community's sake, and the future of generations like little Gethin."

Sian's eyes shone with admiration and she leaned in closer, her voice barely above a whisper.

"You are an inspiration, Rhys Davies. And I believe in you, with all my heart."

Their faces were mere inches apart, and for a moment, the world around them faded away. But the sound of approaching footsteps broke the spell, and they reluctantly pulled apart, their hearts racing with the intensity of the moment.

Rhys swiftly disappeared outside, leaving Sian to be jolted back to reality by Ebba's questioning about the ten boxes of bandages she was supposed to unpack.

"One day, we'll find out who's sending these puzzling monthly donations, Gwen," Ebba declared. "And when we do, we'll have to convince them to send twice as much!"

Gwen turned away, not wanting to give any indication that she might know more than she was letting on.

As Rhys walked down the lane, his mind churned with plans for and against the strike. It was time to test the waters and see if anyone else had an appetite for open rebellion.

CHAPTER 22

That night, under the cover of darkness, Rhys and his father gathered a select group of miners in a secluded corner of the village. The men huddled together, their faces illuminated by the flickering light of a single lantern. Rhys could feel the weight of their gazes on him, expecting him to lead the discussion. He took a deep breath, steadying his nerves.

> "We have to do something," he began, his voice low but firm. "The company is taking advantage of us and we can't take it anymore. No one here would disagree that the Llanwryl crew left all the difficult work to us. Did we get proper recognition for that sacrifice? No."

Murmurs of agreement rippled through the group. Owen nodded in approval.

> "We need to strike," Rhys continued, his voice growing stronger. "We need to show them that we won't be treated as slaves any longer. But we must be smart about it. We can't just walk out and leave our families to starve. We need to plan and act strategically."

The men nodded, understanding the gravity of the situation.

> "What do you propose we do?" asked Tom.

Owen and Rhys exchanged a loaded glance before Rhys spoke again.

> "We organise. We stand together. As one. And if necessary, we strike. It's the only way to make them listen, to force them to treat us with the dignity and respect we deserve. We owe it to the men and boys who lost their lives down in that treacherous pit to fight for a better future for us. For all miners across Britain. Who's with me?"

A nervous murmur of assent rippled through the group, and Rhys felt a surge of pride at the bravery and resolve of his fellow miners. They were embarking on a perilous mission that could cost them everything, but he knew in his heart that it was the right thing to do.

As the conspirators melted into the night, Rhys lingered for a moment, his gaze fixed on the distant silhouette of the mine's winding gear against the starry moonlit sky.

The battle lines had been drawn, and the fate of Cwmgryf hung in the balance. But with the love of their families and the unwavering support of the community behind them, Rhys Davies was convinced that anything was possible.

CHAPTER 23

Only a fortnight had passed since the mine reopened, and already the miners' patience was wearing thin.

Rhys Davies stood before the gathered crowd at the Working Men's Club, his muscular frame taut with tension, atop of the low stage in the hall normally reserved for the brass bands and travelling acts.

> "Men, it's clear that Huntingdon ain't going to budge an inch to help us. He's as selfish as ever, still lining his pockets while we break our backs. And what sticks in my throat is that it's on top of all that voluntary work we did to save his mine and our jobs. He'd be floundering without us stepping in. We're still lacking enough safety lamps. And, yes, a new ventilation shaft has been fitted, but the fans keep breaking, rendering them nigh on useless. I could go on—"

Murmurs of agreement rippled through the room.

> "It's time we take a stand. A strike, to force his hand and make him see reason."

Owen Davies stepped up, and put an arm around his son's shoulder, to show his support.

> "Rhys is right. Elliot and the Reverend amongst others have tried talking to the man, but Charles simply won't listen. A strike is our only hope if

we're going to get a proper wage, and better conditions."

From the stage, Rhys scanned each and every pair of eyes in the room.

"Who's with us?" he yelled, punching the air in anger.

A chorus of *'Aye!'* filled the air as the miners raised their fists in solidarity. Rhys felt a surge of pride at their unity, even as uncertainty gnawed at his gut.

Despite the secrecy of the planned strike, news quickly spread throughout Cwmgryf and the surrounding valleys, whispered in hushed tones. Leaders from various mining communities gathered in Rhys's clandestine meetings, enticed by the young man's charismatic style and the alluring promise of radical change and a better life for all.

*

After another exhausting day, Ebba and Elliot lay in bed discussing the colliery dispute with growing concern.

"A strike?" Ebba whispered. "Do they know what it means? The government will deploy troops to quell the unrest, like they did in Llanelli. Two men dead, Elliot."

Her troubled husband nodded grimly.

"It is not really our battle, Ebba. As my parents told us, all we should do is continue to offer our support to this community. Help them weather the storm until Huntingdon comes to his senses and at least considers talking to them properly again. I'll pay him another visit tomorrow, maybe ask Reverend Jenkins to attend to diffuse the situation a little."

"Well, whatever you do decide to do, I don't think you can make the situation worse, my love."

*

Despite the wintery conditions, Elliot set out to reason with Huntingdon, accompanied by the revered Reverend Jenkins. There they found the mine owner in his opulent office as usual, surrounded by ledgers, looking for every penny to pinch.

"Mr Huntingdon, please, the trust understands your frustration that the mine repairs were expensive, and your quarterly production has tumbled since the accident," Elliot implored, "however, the men proved their loyalty by helping to fix the mine—a job that normally takes weeks - in days. They have legitimate grievances about the working practices, like many miners up and down the land. Surely we can find a compromise."

Huntingdon scoffed, his eyes cold.

"Compromise? I'm running a business, not a charity like you. I have suffered too, paying for those repairs out of my own personal savings. They should be thankful they have jobs at all."

Reverend Jenkins interrupted, his voice calm but firm.

"Mr Huntingdon, speaking on behalf of the Christians in this parish, we have a duty to treat our fellow man with compassion and fairness. The Bible teaches us—"

"Spare me your sermons, Reverend," Huntingdon snapped.

"My only duty is to my shareholders and my profits. Now, if you'll excuse me, I have urgent work to do."

Elliot and Reverend Jenkins left wondering if the deadlock would ever be broken.

"So be it, Reverend. If Huntingdon won't see reason, we'll have to find other ways to help. And I know just who to ask.

*

Elliot Chadwick read his freshly penned letter to Ebba to gauge her opinion.

Salvation Army Headquarters
101 Queen Victoria Street
London

Dear Mr Booth,

I hope this letter finds you in good spirits. I am Elliot Chadwick, son of one of London's Commanding Officers, Mr John Chadwick.

I am writing to you today from the heart of the South Wales coalfields, where a storm is brewing that threatens to engulf our communities in hardship and suffering. The miners of Cwmgryf are on the brink of a strike, their grievances deep-seated and their resolve unwavering.

As the leader of the joint operation between the Salvation Army and the Miner's Benevolent Trust in Glamorgan, I have witnessed firsthand the toll that neglect, poverty and deprivation takes on the health and well-being of these people. The horrific explosion just over a month ago, killing twenty three souls, along with the strain of getting the mine operational again, has worsened labour relations and a strike looms.

This will undoubtedly lead to a loss of wages further exacerbating the existing hardships endured by these poor individuals.

My heart aches for the most vulnerable in our community: young children, the elderly, the injured, and those fighting chronic respiratory illnesses. These individuals are unable to work through no fault of their own and depend on meagre income from their menfolk or the benevolent trust to survive.

A prolonged strike will have devastating consequences for their health and well-being.

Worse still, there is the matter of dealing with the rallies and picketing. I dread the thought of the government sending in troops or the police to quell any uprising. Having read about escalating violence at many collieries across our fair nation, it feels only a matter of time before more lives are lost here.

I know that the Salvation Army, under your compassionate leadership, has a long and noble history of providing assistance to those in need. I am confident that something can be done before the situation deteriorates further.

Thank you for your time and consideration. I eagerly await your response and pray for your guidance in this urgent matter.

Yours sincerely,

Elliot Chadwick

The Glamorgan Miner's Benevolent Trust

*

Despite sporadic attempts at reconciliation, industrial relations at the Cwmgryf colliery continued to deteriorate. The miners grew increasingly frustrated with each passing day as they continued to face dangerous working conditions. The breaking point finally arrived when Tom Watts lost two fingers, crushed by a runaway coal cart towards the end of his twelve-hour shift.

Adding fuel to the fire, rumours began to circulate that Huntingdon had instructed Gerald Price to tamper with the weighing scales, causing every hewer's sack to be under-weighed.

This act of deceit was the final straw for many, particularly Rhys Davies, who had been carefully monitoring the situation and gathering evidence to present when the time was right.

*

At the end of a particularly gruelling shift, Rhys stood before a crowd of miners gathered near the pithead. His voice, filled with passion and determination, rang out across the assembled workers.

> "Brothers, we've endured enough!" he declared, his fists clenched at his sides. "We've given our sweat, our blood, and even our lives to this mine. And how does Huntingdon repay us? With disrespect and deceit! When was cheating us at the scales, robbing us of our hard-earned wages, ever going to be acceptable?"

Murmurs of agreement rippled through the crowd as Rhys continued.

> "Tom Watts lost his fingers because the long hours have utterly exhausted him. How many more injuries —deaths even—must we suffer before we are taken seriously and our lives valued?"

The miners' anger was palpable, their expressions a mixture of rage and determination.

> "I say enough is enough!" Rhys shouted, his voice rising with emotion. "It's time we take a stand."

A roar of approval erupted from the crowd, and Rhys seized the moment.

> "I call for a strike!" he declared, his voice carrying across the throng. "We will not return to work until our demands for safer conditions and fair pay are met. Who's with me?"

The response was overwhelming. Miners thrust their fists into the air, their voices joining in a thunderous roar of agreement.

The strike had begun.

*

That evening, Elizabeth tried to reason with her husband Charles about how he ran the mine.

"Surely all this acrimony can't be good for business? There must be something you can do?"

"My dear, the challenges we face in this industry are many. It is clear to me the golden age of coal seems to be fading as new energy sources like oil, gas and electricity gain prominence. There's less demand for our product, and foreign competition is fierce. They can mine and transport coal more cheaply than we can, undercutting our prices.

To make matters worse, the veins we've been working for centuries are becoming depleted. It's increasingly difficult and costly to extract the coal that remains. We have to dig deeper and further, invest in new machinery, more water pumps and supports, and hire more experienced miners. This, of course, drives up our expenses.

Additionally, the government has imposed stricter safety regulations in the wake of several mining disasters. While I believe safety is paramount, these regulations require substantial investments in ventilation systems, safety equipment, and training programmes.

And now there's the ever-present threat of labour unrest. The miners are demanding higher wages and better working conditions, which is understandable given the dangerous nature of their work. However, meeting their demands further erodes our already thin profit margins.

Taken together, these factors have created a perfect storm of challenges that threaten the very viability of our colliery. It's a difficult situation with no easy solutions, and no winners."

"But the men deserve more. You deserve more," Elizabeth countered. "This is no life for you. Swallow your pride, Charles. Fix the mine. Sell the mine. Or close it."

Charles was livid about his options, but that didn't change the fact they were the only choices he had.

CHAPTER 24

As news of the strike spread through the valley and out to Glamorgan, it wasn't just the men who were mobilising. Sian Williams, with young Gethin nestled in her shawl, stood tall on the village green, addressing a gathering of women she had managed to mobilise, thanks to a handwritten poster in Mrs Morgan's shop.

> "We must stand together, sisters! Our husbands, our fathers, our brothers, our sons—they volunteered their labour for a better future for all of us. It's time we played our part—a real part—not just running the household. Ladies, we can do more. Much more. I will not let my Gethin's death be in vain. We must speak up for those whose lives were cut short by Charles Huntingdon so we can protect the men who survived."

A sea of perplexed faces looked back at her, so radical was the suggestion.

> "Like the other women in striking mining communities, we must organise our collective efforts to provide support for the families in most need. We must form committees to raise funds, and coordinate relief efforts. We must maintain community spirit and solidarity.
>
> Women have joined picket lines before, and we shall follow in their footsteps. We must not be

afraid to challenge those in authority, and like the menfolk, we must demand better conditions for our families and communities. Together, we can make this strike both more bearable and be swiftly resolved. Our menfolk must not suffer alone."

The women's faces began to turn from puzzled to emboldened by possibility.

Sian swelled with pride as she gazed upon these resilient and oppressed souls who had already endured so much, who still displayed a willingness to face even more challenges. Rhys's unwavering faith in her had motivated the young widow. Now, Mrs Sian Williams was the champion of the women of Cwmgryf.

Sian's words ignited a flame in the hearts of the village women, and they quickly banded together to support the strike. They formed groups with different focuses. Some gathered and distributed donated food. Others arranged childcare for more women to join the fight. A group of older women took charge of knitting warm clothes for those protesting in all kinds of weather at the picket line.

Sian tirelessly organised their efforts and ensured no family went without support. She held daily meetings at eleven, where women could share information, voice concerns, and uplift each other's spirits.

The bond between these women grew stronger with each passing day. Soon, Sian organised the women into shifts to maintain a strong presence on the picket lines. They marched alongside their men, chanting and singing in unison, a united force against injustice.

Like their sisters in Merthyr Tydfil, Aberdare, and the Rhondda, the sight of the women of Cwmgryf standing shoulder to shoulder with their men brought new determination to their cause, inspiring even the most downtrodden and sickly miners to stand firm.

The women's unwavering support set journalists' hands on fire as they frantically typed away, desperate to break the story first. Each word flowed like molten lava, fuelled by the passion and determination of these resilient women.

Charles Huntingdon would not be influenced so easily, however.

*

It had taken a few days to secure the extra manpower, but soon the first of the black legs arrived to break the strike—none other than the Llanwryl men who'd helped repair the mine.

Sian watched in disbelief as the men marched towards the picket lines, pickaxes in hand, their faces set in grim determination. The betrayal cut deep, especially since some of the men had bonded over a pint.

"Scabs!" Rhys shouted, his face contorted with rage. "Traitors to your own kind!"

The picket line surged forward, tempers boiling over. Sian watched in horror as the two sides clashed, fists flying, curses echoing in the air. She clutched Gethin tightly to her chest, desperate to shield him from the violence erupting around them. *'Is this what our world has come to? Brother against brother, neighbour against neighbour?'*

As the melee intensified, Sian found herself torn between her instinct to protect her child and her desire to stand with the striking men and women. She saw widows she had rallied now caught up in the thick of the fight. The unity she had worked so hard to build was being tested in the crucible of conflict.

Suddenly, a piercing whistle cut through the noise. A swarm of police officers began to push through the crowd, roughly separating the warring factions. Sian saw several miners being dragged away under arrest, their faces bloodied and defiant, their women folk trying to cling onto them but failing.

Eventually, the black legs had fought their way into the mine, its entrance now flanked by eight burly policemen, all recruited by Huntingdon to keep the mine open—whatever the personal or economic cost.

*

As the dust settled, Sian realised that this was only the beginning. The strike had taken a violent turn within days, and the road ahead would be far more treacherous than any of them had imagined. But as she looked around at the determined faces of her fellow villagers, she knew that they would face whatever came next together.

Exhausted, hungry, and worried for little Gethin, but with an unbroken spirit, Sian headed to the safety of the clinic.

She arrived to find Elliot speaking to Reverend Jenkins and some other members of the trust about the escalating violence, and planning support for those who had been arrested. The women's committees sprang into action like a blaze of phoenixes, proving that their conviction, preparation and mobilisation effort could easily match the men.

*

The battle lines had been drawn again. Huntingdon showed no sign of wanting a peaceful solution. The black legs would be back tomorrow.

The beleaguered people of the village were steeling themselves for a long and bitter struggle.

CHAPTER 25

Gerald Price lurked in the shadows, his eyes narrowing as he watched women carrying armfuls of produce across the green to the clinic's makeshift soup kitchen. As the strike dragged on day after day, more families and widows were left in dire straits. It should have been the perfect opportunity for a man like Price to exploit their vulnerability. He was most unhappy that these women were providing aid to those in need.

He stepped forward and approached a small party of women heading to the picket line, his voice dripping with false concern.

> "Ladies, I couldn't help but overhear your worries about the future. With the union's strike fund due to run dry soon, I fear many of you may soon find yourselves without a roof over your heads. You can't expect Mr Huntingdon to let you stay in his cottages only to help wreak havoc on his colliery. He's within his rights to evict you, you know?"

The women, many of them widows, exchanged anxious glances. Gerald smiled, a predatory glint in his eye.

> "Of course, I may be able to help convince Charles to let you stay— for a price."

He let his gaze linger on each woman in turn, his meaning all too clear.

"Think it over, ladies. You know where to find me."

With that, he turned and strode away, leaving a chill in the air that had nothing to do with the wintry air.

*

Word quickly spread about Gerald's sinister actions, reaching the ears of the Chadwicks.

"It's utterly despicable," Ebba fumed, her footsteps echoing as she paced the length of the clinic. "Gerald Price, preying on these vulnerable women, forcing them into unspeakable acts just for the mere hope of keeping a roof over their heads. And even then, there's no guarantee he'll keep his word. I fear Sian's awful experience in the shop was just the tip of the iceberg. Have you noticed how withdrawn some of the widows have become lately?

It can't all be attributed to the colliery violence. There's something more insidious at work here, Elliot, and we need to put a stop to it."

Elliot nodded grimly, his own anger simmering just beneath the surface.

"We need proof though. The police won't act without it. I'll see if Gwen can get them to confide in her. She can explain the importance of physical evidence," Elliot said, his voice steady. "We'll gather testimonies from the women and document any signs of abuse. We'll build a case against Gerald that even sceptical authorities can't ignore. He needs to be behind bars."

As Gwen set out on her secret mission, Ebba couldn't shake the uneasy feeling in her stomach. It had been weeks since the explosion—how many women had fallen victim to Gerald's advances since? And how many more would suffer before he was brought to justice? With few laws protecting them and society automatically believing men over women, keeping these women safe would be a challenge.

Memories of her past flooded Ebba's mind—the mistreatment by Arthur McAlistair still lingering. She could feel his unwanted touch and hear his threats ringing in her ears. The fear she felt sleeping in Molly's room to escape his nighttime visits, the pain from his brutal beatings that left her barely able to see. She shuddered at the thought, remembering how he used her father's criminal past to manipulate her. But she had promised herself to never let anyone else suffer as she had. Now was the time to keep that promise.

*

The harsh winter wind continued to whip through the narrow lanes of Cwmgryf, carrying with it the bitter chill of long-term desperation. Ebba pulled her coat tighter around her shoulders as she hurried towards the clinic, her mind weighed down by the troubles that seemed to multiply with each passing day.

'Two months,' she thought grimly. 'Two months since the strike began, and still no end in sight.'

She could see the toll it was taking on the village—gaunt faces of the miners, hollow eyes of their wives and children. The once-bustling streets were now eerily quiet, save for occasional scuffles between strikers and strikebreakers. The icy weather made picketing even more unbearable during shorter days and longer nights.

Generosity from the public was waning. Fundraising grew more frustrating and fruitless by the day.

As she neared the clinic, a commotion caught her attention. A group of men huddled around the back, their whispered voices rising in anger. Ebba quickened her pace, her heart sinking as she recognised the scene all too well.

> "Elliot! Come quickly! Elliot! Gwen! Somebody please help!"

The back door slammed against the wall accompanied by footsteps.

> "Oi! What do you think you're doing?" Elliot shouted, grabbing back a sack of coal from the thief. "That's for the clinic, not you!"

> "My family's freezing, mate. We've got no choice."

Ebba stepped forward, her voice calm but firm.

> "Gentlemen, please. There's no need for all this aggression. I know it's hard," she said softly. "But stealing, poaching, and whatever else you are doing will only make things worse. The authorities are cracking down harder than ever."

As if on cue, the sound of marching feet echoed through the street. A group of policemen rounded the corner, their batons at the ready. The other men scattered, but the man nearest to Elliot stumbled over the coal sack. The thief was quickly encircled, and batons rained down on him. Then he was dragged away, kicking and screaming all the way to the policemen's black maria.

Ebba watched them go, a heavy weight settling on her chest. 'How much longer can this go on?' she wondered. 'How much more can these people endure?'

She thought of the strike fund, dwindling by the day as more and more families struggled to make ends meet. Of the soup kitchens she and Elliot had set up, stretched thin by the sheer number of hungry mouths to feed.

'We need help,' she realised with a sinking feeling. 'We can't do this alone.'

As Gwen entered the clinic, she looked up from her work, her brow furrowed with concern.

> "Is everything alright, Ebba? You look troubled?" her friend asked.

She nodded sympathetically as she listened.

"It's hard, seeing everyone suffer like this. But we'll get through it, somehow. We always do. By the way, we had another mystery delivery this afternoon."

Ebba managed a small smile.

"Another one?" she asked, hardly daring to believe it.

"Triple the usual amount this time," said Gwen. "Seems you've got a very generous benefactor, Dr Chadwick."

"Was there a note? Anything to help us work out who it is?"

"Nothing—" Who could it be, Gwen? Who would give so much, so consistently, without even sharing their name?"

"Ahh!"

"What?"

"There's a note. Here at the bottom of the box, Gwen."

"Oh yes, I couldn't make out what it meant. Can you help me decipher it?" said Gwen awkwardly.

Gwen shifted her weight from foot to foot, avoiding Ebba's gaze as she tried to make sense of the message. Saying nothing, the midwife busied herself with unpacking the boxes. As Ebba watched her, a nagging suspicion started to take root in her mind. 'Gwen knows something. Something she's not telling me. Otherwise, she'd help me work out what this message means!' But before she could press further, a miner with a bloodied face and a wild look in his eyes appeared and the questioning would have to wait.

> "Ebba, Elliot, come quick! There's been another fight at the picket line between the men and the blacklegs. Owen took a bad blow to the head."

The next morning dawned cold and grey, the air thick with tension and anticipation. As the miners gathered at the colliery gates, Rhys scanned the crowd for Sian, his heart in his throat. 'She shouldn't be here.' But there she was, Gethin clutched to her chest, her face pale but determined.

> "What are you doing here? You should be at home. The fighting last night was brutal," Rhys exclaimed.

Sian shook her head stubbornly.

> "I can't just sit by and do nothing, Rhys. This is my fight too. Our fight."

> Suddenly, a shout went up from the picket line. "Blacklegs! The blacklegs are coming!"

Rhys whirled around, his heart sinking as he saw the group of men approaching the gates, their faces hard and unfriendly. The strikers surged forward, their anger boiling over into shouts and curses. The strike-breakers responded in kind, their own voices rising in a cacophony of rage and defiance.

In the midst of the chaos, Sian clutched her baby tighter, her eyes wide with fear. Rhys moved to shield her with his body, but it was too late.

A rock, hurled from the crowd, struck Sian in the head. She staggered, her grip on the baby loosening as she fell to the ground.

> "Sian!" Rhys screamed, lunging forward to catch her. But before he could reach her, the crowd surged again, trampling everything in its path.

Rhys watched in horror as Sian disappeared beneath a sea of bodies, the baby's cries drowned out by the roar of the mob. He fought his way forward, his heart pounding with terror and desperation.

And then, miraculously, he saw a flash of a familiar face pushing through the crowd. It was Gwen, her arms outstretched, reaching for Sian and the baby. With a burst of strength, Gwen surged forward, grabbing Sian's arm and pulling her to her feet. Together, they stumbled clear of the mob, Gwen cradling the wailing infant to her chest.

> "Thank you," Sian gasped, tears streaming down her face. "Thank you, Gwen. I don't know what I would have done—"

Gwen smiled grimly, her own eyes brimming with unshed tears.

"We look out for each other, love. That's what we do in Cwmgryf."

Rhys wanted to pull Sian and Gethin into him, protect them, his heart still racing with fear and relief. *'That was too damn close.'*

CHAPTER 26

The air in Cwmgryf was thick with the coal dust that hung over the village like a grim shroud, settling into every crevice and wrinkle. Gwen stood by the window of her uncle's cottage, her fingers tracing the rough wooden frame as she looked out onto the grimy cobbled street that led to the picket line flanking the colliery. It was meant to be a happier time with her mariner fiancé at her side, but things felt as unbearable as ever.

"It's been a month, Llewellyn," Gwen said, her voice a mixture of resignation and determination.

"Another horrible month—and still no end in sight."

Llewellyn's strong arms encircled her from behind, his touch both comforting and firm.

"Aye, love. It's a hard time for everyone. I've been asking round the docks to see if there's any more shipping work. I can't see the mine staying open much longer?"

"You think so? What will Uncle Ifan do? His cough is so bad I don't know how much longer he can keep going." she replied, turning to face him.

"He's deteriorated since the strikes began. The uncertainty— it's too much for him. He's not coming for soup. He lies in bed like he's waiting for the end to come."

Gwen looked over to his bed, Ifan fast asleep, looking like a skeleton under a shroud.

"He's a tough old soul," Llewellyn said, though the concern in his voice betrayed his words. "But you're right. The strike's taken a toll on all of us."

"Do you think we should postpone the wedding altogether? We don't know what we're doing from one week to the next. And there's less coal for you to ship to London. What happens when there's none?" Gwen asked, the question weighing heavily on her heart.

Llewellyn sighed, his brow furrowing.

"I hate the thought, but it might be wise. With everything so uncertain— it's not the time to be starting our new life together. Especially if we take your uncle with us."

He paused, then added softly:

"We'll find our moment, Gwen. Just not yet."

Gwen nodded, feeling a pang of disappointment mixed with relief.

"You're right. We need to focus on getting through this first."

*

Later that afternoon, Gwen wrapped her shawl tightly around her shoulders and made her way to an imposing country house on the hill. The path was familiar, each step taken with the same old secrecy. She looked about then snuck around to the servant's entrance and let herself in.

A glance at the kitchen clock confirmed the impeccable timing of her visit. Silently, she slipped along the servant corridors to the guest bedroom, only making a slight noise as she knocked on the door.

> "Come in, Gwen," a voice beckoned from inside as the heavy door creaked open.

Stepping into the warmth, Gwen couldn't help but feel like she was in a different world compared to the miners' cottages. Soft carpets, marble fireplaces, paintings of ancestors and landscapes adorned the walls, with a faint scent of dried lavender lingering in the air.

> "Thank you, Mrs Huntington," Gwen replied gratefully, following Elizabeth to the small desk where she had been working. "I don't think anyone saw me."

> "Excellent," Elizabeth said with a relieved smile. "We must be careful. If Charles finds out you've been here, it could spell trouble for us."

As they settled down to talk, Elizabeth leaned forward with earnest expression.

"Do you have a list of what the clinic needs this month?"

"Yes," Gwen nodded, pulling out a crumpled piece of paper from her pocket. "We need more coal for heating. It's locked away now, but it still gets stolen sometimes. You can't blame the villagers though—this winter weather has added significantly to their struggles. Maybe we can arrange for smaller deliveries so we won't lose all of it if it does get stolen? And our stock of essentials for making soup is running low after some root vegetables rotted in the cold and damp conditions. The Chadwick's only light and heat certain rooms to conserve fuel. Do you think there's a way we can secure more supplies?"

"I'm afraid my secret inheritance is running low, Gwen," Elizabeth confessed, her voice tinged with worry. "We have three months left at best, and I dare not ask those sympathetic to the villagers' plight to contribute further."

She paused, her eyes filled with a mix of compassion and determination.

"As Christians, we are taught, 'When I was hungry, you gave me food; when I was thirsty, you gave me drink; when I was a stranger, you welcomed me.' I cannot, in good conscience, stand by and do nothing while our community suffers."

Elizabeth's expression grew serious as she continued.

"However, Gwen, it is imperative that no one discovers my involvement. Our family name is already tarnished, and I fear Charles would seek a divorce if he knew I was easing the burden on the miners. He would undoubtedly view it as a betrayal—an act that prolonged the strike and undermined his authority."

Gwen's heart sank.

"What will we do then?"

"Let's make every penny count," Elizabeth replied, her resolve unwavering. "We can help them get through the worst of it. After that, we'll pray for better times. There has to be an end to the strike soon—few run beyond a month or two."

"I appreciate the sacrifice you are making. You're a godsend, Mrs Huntington."

"Call me Elizabeth," she said with a soft smile. "After all, we're in this together."

As Gwen left Huntingdon Hall, the weight of their conversation pressed heavily upon her. The pretty evening sky was tinged with hues of pink and orange—a deceptive beauty masking the hardships of the village below. She quickened her pace, her thoughts consumed by the dwindling funds, the dear faces of lifelong friends and acquaintances who depended on the handouts, and what she would do if she had to move away.

Back at the cottage, Llewellyn awaited her return, his figure silhouetted against the dim light of the hearth.

"How did it go?"

"The clinic is as busy as ever, Llew. I've left Sian to help hold the fort.—Are you awake, uncle? Ebba's sent you some soup to keep your strength up. Potato and leek."

"Oh, my favourite," Ifan said. "Be a dear and bring it over to me, my love."

As the couple looked at the frail man in the bed struggling to sit up, almost too weak to feed himself, neither of them had the stomach to broach the subject of their still on-off wedding plans when the shadow of sleep dozed off.

The next day, Gwen's conscience burned an even bigger hole in her soul as she trundled past Mrs Morgan's shop and waved at Sian stocking the upper shelves more easily these days.

"How can I keep Elizabeth's secret from Ebba?" Gwen muttered under her breath, her heart heavy with the burden of secrecy. "But I can't risk Charles finding out—or Gerald!"

The thought of her cousin Gerald discovering Elizabeth's clandestine aid sent a shiver down her spine. He would put an end to it immediately and make sure Elizabeth paid for her actions.

"Morning, Gwen," called the shopkeeper, as she put out her wares in front of the shop. "You look like you've got the world on your shoulders."

"Just tired, Mrs Morgan," Gwen replied with a forced smile. "Busy day ahead."

"You and the others need to rest at some point. I'm sure Sian could fall asleep standing up behind the counter."

As Gwen reached Ebba's consultation room door, she paused, taking a deep breath. Surely Ebba could be trusted? She deserved to know where the help was coming from, and that it would soon come to an end so she could plan accordingly. She lifted her hand to knock but hesitated, her knuckles hovering just inches from the worn wood.

The weight of the secret weighed heavily on her mind. She knew Ebba needed to know, but she also couldn't bear the thought of betraying Elizabeth's trust. Her conscience was torn between doing what was right and protecting a friend. She bit her lip, unsure of what to do next.

Before Gwen could resolve her inner turmoil, the door swung open, revealing Ebba's warm, wrinkled face.

"Gwen, love! Come in, come in. You look frozen stiff."

"Thank you, Ebba," Gwen said, stepping inside and feeling the immediate warmth of the hearth.

"Sit yourself down and warm up," Ebba urged, bustling about to fetch a pot of tea. "You look like you've got something on your mind."

"Ebba," Gwen began, her voice faltering. "There's something I need to talk to you about."

"What? Has something happened?"

"No. Well, yes. But no," Gwen rambled as her heart pounded. "It's about—"

She hesitated, the words tangled in her throat.

Could she really betray Elizabeth's trust?

"About what, dear?" Ebba pressed gently, pouring steaming tea into two enamel cups.

"The thing is—" Gwen started again, but the sound of heavy footsteps on the porch silenced her.

A frantic knock followed, the door creaking open before Ebba could respond.

"Miss Ebba!" a miner burst in, his face pale and eyes wide with distress. "It's my boy—he's sick, coughing blood. Please, you must come!"

"Of course," Ebba replied instantly, rising to her feet. "I'll get my bag."

"Go on," Gwen encouraged, feeling let off the hook for a while. "We'll talk later."

CHAPTER 27

Gerald Price stood outside the colliery office, a smug smirk playing on his lips. In his hands, he clutched a stack of eviction notices, the ink still wet from the press. The power he felt holding these papers was intoxicating—each notice representing another family thrown into chaos and another opportunity for him to exert control over the women and torment the men.

'Ah, the sweet taste of authority,' he mused, strolling towards the miners' cottages. *'Nothing quite like it.'*

He knocked sharply on the first door, relishing the fear that spread across Mrs Watts' face as she opened it.

"Eviction notice," he announced almost cheerfully, thrusting the paper into her shaking hands.

"Please, Mr Price," she begged, tears welling up in her eyes. "We have nowhere else to go."

"Not my concern," Gerald replied coldly, stepping back to admire his handiwork as she slumped against the doorframe.

"You shouldn't have encouraged your husband to strike. You have until the end of the week."

"Heartless monster," she whispered, clutching the notice.

"Just doing my job, unlike some people, Mrs Davies," he responded, moving on to the next house without a second glance.

At each stop, he took perverse pleasure in the fear and desperation written on the faces of those he served. For Gerald, it was more than just delivering bad news—it was a chance to remind everyone who held the real power in Cwmgryf.

"Here you go, Mr Pritchard," he said to an elderly miner barely able to stand without support. "Best start packing since your son prefers the picket line to the coal seam."

"Curse you, Price," Pritchard spat, but Gerald merely laughed, the sound echoing through the narrow street.

"Pleasure doing business."

As he continued his rounds, Gerald's thoughts turned to the inevitable chaos his letters would cause. The miners' flagging spirits would break under the strain. And when they finally caved in and returned to work, he'd be there to witness their defeat as he handed out their tally tags.

"Let them rage," Gerald thought, his smirk widening. "In the end, they'll all bow to Charles. And me."

With the last notice delivered, he walked back towards the colliery, whistling a tune that seemed to mock the suffering of the beleaguered village.

Out on the doorsteps, notices fluttered in the grasp of many trembling hands, their ominous words echoing in every household. Miners gathered in clusters on the picket line, wondering how to respond.

"How can Charles do this to us?" Owen Davies roared, crumpling his eviction notice in his grimy hand. "After all we've sacrificed in the past? Now is the time to fight back harder."

"Shut up, Owen," Tom Watts muttered angrily, casting a wary glance around. "We don't need any more trouble."

"More trouble? We're being tossed out like rubbish!" Owen's anger was palpable, his eyes blazing with defiance. "Where are we supposed to go?"

"Back to work, perhaps," came a resigned voice from the back—John Hughes, one of the older miners who could still work. "Maybe it's time to give in."

"Give in?" Owen snapped, turning to face him. "And let them win? Let that devil Price and Huntingdon trample over us even more? They'll know they have the upper hand. Nothing good will come of it until Huntingdon changes his tune."

"Caving in is better than seeing our families on the streets in winter," John retorted, his tone weary but firm. "We've fought hard, but what has it brought us? Nothing but even more misery and hunger. The repairs may not be great, but they are serviceable. And Price can fix the scales, if he knows what's good for him."

A heavy silence fell over the group as each man grappled with his own turmoil. The desperation in their eyes mirrored the bleakness of the grey sky above.

"Look at us," Tom said, his voice softer now, tinged with hopelessness. "Reduced to begging for scraps. This strike— it feels like we're fighting a losing battle."

"Maybe we are," whispered another miner, his face shadowed by the brim of his cap. "Time to face it lads, I say."

As if in answer, a loud clanging ending the black legs shift broke the stillness. All heads turned towards the colliery gates, where a few men were daubing crude, angry insults in white paint. 'Huntingdon starves our children for his own greed.' and much worse.

"That won't help," John sighed, shaking his head.

"It'll only enrage him more."

"Let them see our fury," Owen replied, his jaw set. "They need to know we won't be silenced."

"Fury won't feed our children," John countered.

"Nor will it keep a roof over our heads."

"Then what, John?" Tom asked, desperation creeping into his voice. "What do we do? We're not making ends meet when we do work!"

The tension among the group was thick, each man wrestling with the impossible choices before them.

"Price is enjoying this," muttered Owen, his eyes narrowing as he stared at the gate. "He loves watching us squirm. That's why we can't give in. Not yet. Let's sleep on it. Take a vote in the morning?"

"Right or wrong," Tom said, his voice barely a whisper, "it feels like we're trapped."

One by one, the men drifted away, their steps heavy and uncertain.

*

As the moon rose high in the sky, Gwen sat by the window, her fingers deftly working on a piece of embroidery. Though her mind was far from the delicate flowers taking shape beneath her needle.

"Love," Llewellyn's voice broke through her reverie as he entered the front room. "We need to talk."

"Aye, we do," she replied, setting down her work. She rose and moved towards him, her hands finding comfort in his rough, calloused ones.

"Shall we sit?" he suggested, nodding towards the small wooden bench that had seen countless meals and heartfelt discussions over the years.

"Uncle Ifan's cough is getting worse," Llewellyn began, concern evident in his voice. "I took him to see Elliot. It's not just the cold and damp of this old place affecting him. It's those years down the mine, I'm afraid."

"He's been like a father to me, Llew," Gwen said softly, tears welling in her eyes. "I can't bear the thought of him in the workhouse."

Llewellyn sighed, running a hand through his wavy hair.

"I know, Gwennie. But there's a chance for us—out there. Away from Cwmgryf and the mines. We could have a better life. And I hate to say this, but Ifan won't be with us forever. And if Elliot's diagnosis is correct—well, I'm sorry love, but he doesn't have long."

Gwen's eyes fell and her lower lip trembled.

"Where would we go?" she asked in a barely audible whisper. "To some other city's docks where no one knows us? Where we'd just be another struggling couple? With no friends to rely on?"

"Maybe," Llewellyn admitted, leaning closer. "But we could make something of ourselves. Find honest work. New work. Live without the constant fear of strikes and evictions. Every town needs midwives. And I can turn my hand to quite a few different trades, not just sailing. Ship building. Ship repair? Fitting rigging. Lots of things."

"Fine. But leaving Uncle Ifan isn't an option," Gwen said firmly, though her heart ached at the thought. "Who would care for him? Who would make sure he has his medicine, his food? I can't ask Ebba. If he lives, I must stay to care for him. And if he passes, well—you can't stay with me when you're on leave. People will talk."

"Yes, you're right," Llewellyn conceded, squeezing her hand. "But what future do we have here, carrying on like this? The strikes are tearing this place apart. We need a plan."

"There's no easy answer, is there?" Gwen murmured, resting her head on his shoulder.

"We're trapped between our duty to family and our hope for a better life. Stuck in a place doing its best to crush us."

"Whatever we decide," Llewellyn said softly, kissing her forehead, "we'll face it together. I love you, Gwen, and for now, that's all that matters."

Outside, the wind picked up, carrying the faint sounds of raised voices and hurried footsteps. The village was a powder keg, ready to explode at the slightest spark.

CHAPTER 28

"Rhys, we can't hold out much longer," Owen said with a heavy voice, feeling the weight of their predicament as the flickering light from the oil lamp cast long shadows on the walls of their modest dwelling. "Something's got to give, lad."

"I know, Da," Rhys replied, nervously drumming his fingers. "But joining forces with the other striking collieries—it's a gamble. If we fail, it'll be more than just our livelihoods at stake. None of us will work in Glamorgan again."

Owen paused, gazing deeply into his son's eyes for solidarity.

"Do you stand with me? It's Cardiff or bust, son."

"One last stand? Hmm. I reckon it's worth the risk. If we win, we win. If we lose, Huntingdon will pick us over stranger men. He's stubborn but not stupid."

"Together, we might just have a chance." Owen said, feeling a spark of determination reignite within him. "We rally the men, gather every ounce of strength we've got and show the colliery owners we're not beaten yet. One last push."

"Alright, Da," Rhys agreed. "Let's march tomorrow, Sunday."

With the decision made, they clasped hands firmly—father and son united in purpose.

"Better tell the men it won't be chapel for 'em in the morning."

*

The streets of Cardiff were filled with a sea of faces. Always a bustling city, it was now overflowing with miners and their families, all heading towards Victoria Park. Boldly decorated banners fluttered in the breeze, displaying the names of different collieries and the intimidating red dragon of Wales.

Underneath, words proudly proclaimed their values: 'Cwmgryf Colliery—United for Fair Wages!' and 'Remember the Fallen—Safety for All!' One banner simply read 'Solidarity Forever!'

"Brothers!" boomed a voice from the makeshift podium on the wrought-iron bandstand, catching the attention of the crowd. "We've all come here today to have our voices heard!"

It was Idris Davies, the formidable leader of the miners' union from Rhondda Valley. His face was stern and clean-shaven, his dark hair now streaked with grey falling over his forehead. His eyes blazed with passion and determination.

He stood tall and proud, his shoulders squared and fists clenched at his sides. His voice, roughened by coal dust and countless speeches, carried the strength and defiance of all Welsh mining communities.

Rhys stood side by side with Owen, his heart pounding in his chest. The crowd around them surged and cheered as they braved the icy cold air. Despite the discomfort, Rhys could feel the warmth of bodies pressed closely together and hear the murmurs of conversations filled with anger and hope shared between strangers.

> "Today, we stand united against the tyranny of the mine owners!" declared another speaker who took to the stage, his voice clear and powerful. "They think they can break us, but they underestimate our spirit!"

> "He's right," Rhys whispered to Owen, feeling a surge of pride. "We're stronger when we're together."

> "Keep that fire burning, lad," Owen replied, scanning the crowd with his eyes. "We'll need every bit of it if we're going to fight off eviction!"

The speeches continued, each one a call to action and a rallying cry that resonated deeply with the miners. Faces young and old, marked with signs of struggle and hard work, lifted in agreement and defiance. Fists clenched, voices united in chants that filled the streets with a powerful roar.

> "Down with greedy owners! We demand fair wages for all!"

"Justice for the miners! No more starvation!"

"Stand strong, brothers and sisters!"

As the rally reached its climax and prepared to march towards the Miners' Institute, Rhys felt a mix of emotions—hope, fear, determination—all swirling together. The path ahead was treacherous, but for now, they stood unified, a force to be reckoned with. There was a slim chance that their goal of better working conditions could be achieved.

'Whatever comes next we will face it together.'

*

Rhys' heart pounded in his chest as he looked around at the swelling crowd marching through the streets of Cardiff. The onlookers had a mix of curious and disdainful expressions. Uniformed policemen stood in rigid formation along the roads, their stern faces hidden by their bobby helmets.

Behind them, troops loomed with rifles at the ready. The miners' chants echoed through the city, a powerful testament to their collective resolve.

"Fair wages for all!" Rhys shouted, joining in the cacophony. Beside him, Owen's expression was grim but determined, with piercing eyes scanning their surroundings.

"Keep moving, lads," Owen commanded in his Welsh accent. "We can't let 'em intimidate us."

As they marched past St David's Hall towards the castle, the iconic landmarks added gravitas to the unfolding drama. The sense of purpose among the miners was palpable, each step taken despite the weight of their struggle pressing down upon them.

"No more starvation! No more black legs and black lists! No more evictions!" the chant rose again, louder this time and reverberating off the stone facades of buildings.

"Look at 'em, Rhys," Owen muttered, nodding toward the policemen. "The colliery owners have pulled out all the stops, haven't they?"

"Aye," Rhys replied with a clenched jaw. "But we're not backing down. This is our one big chance."

The tension was thick in the air, crackling with potential energy. The march continued as a river of humanity through the city, driven by a shared determination that refused to be quelled.

Then without warning, a scuffle broke out near the front of the march with men planted by the colliery owners causing trouble, while journalists were ready to blame it on the miners in their reports.

Rhys strained to see what was happening, but the mass of placards and banners obstructed his view.

Shouts erupted, followed by the unmistakable sounds of fists, batons, and shields meeting flesh.

The police surged forward with truncheons raised, chaos ensuing. Gunshots were fired into the air.

> "Hold the line!" Owen bellowed, but his voice was drowned out by the uproar.

Rhys felt a surge of panic as mounted police charged into the crowd, their horses rearing up and hooves striking innocent men indiscriminately, causing many to fall like rag dolls.

> "Make way for the women and children!" Owen roared, pushing through the throng to create a path.

But the violence was escalating too quickly. Shop windows were broken and panicked miners began to stampede, trampling on their fallen brothers leaving the braver ones to try and get them back on their feet.

> "Get back!" a policeman shouted, swinging his baton wildly.

Rhys ducked, narrowly avoiding the blow, but the man next to him wasn't so lucky. He went down with a grunt, clutching his head.

"Bryn!" Rhys called out, spotting the stocky miner grappling with an officer.

Bryn's face was a mask of fury, but even he couldn't withstand the onslaught alone. Rhys rushed to his aid, only to be met with a brutal shove that sent him sprawling on the ground.

More gunshots rang out, deafening cracks slicing through the chaos. Windows were shattered and the horses continued to charge. Panic rippled through the entire crowd as people scrambled to escape the violent melee.

Rhys struggled to keep his footing, blood trickling down from his badly cut palms. But he pushed on, his only thought being getting himself and his colleagues to safety.

"Over here, men, ladies!" Owen's voice cut through the madness, guiding the men towards a narrow alley, every step a battle against the crush of bodies.

"Just a bit further," Owen panted, glancing back to ensure they weren't being followed. "We'll regroup and figure out our next move."

Rhys nodded, though his heart was heavy. The reality of their situation was stark and unforgiving.

They had come seeking justice, but found only violence and despair. Giving into Huntingdon's demands was now the only realistic option left. With no savings, and no food, biting the one hand that could still feed the community was not a prudent move.

The time to be stubborn and defiant was gone. Capitulation to the colliery owner's demands was the new order of the day.

CHAPTER 29

As they marched back to the colliery, those who were able to walk did so with solemn procession. It was a stark contrast to the earlier fervour that had driven them to Cardiff. The miners trudged along the muddy paths and lanes, their shoulders slumped under the weight of defeat. Carts creaked under the burden of the injured while those who could hardly stand were escorted to the train station, filling up the carriages.

Rhys walked beside his father, each step a painful reminder of their failure and inevitable surrender. His head throbbed from where it had hit the ground, but it was the ache in his heart that hurt more. Around them, murmurs from the men echoed through the air. They had fought with bravery, but ultimately they were outnumbered and outmatched by their ruthless opposition. The dream of better working conditions seemed farther away than ever.

"Look at 'em," Rhys muttered, glancing at Owen.

"We put our all into this and what do we have to show for it?"

"Bruises and broken bones," Owen replied bitterly.

"But don't think for a moment that our spirit is broken, lad. We may be down, but we ain't out."

"Feels like we're out," Rhys said quietly.

"Maybe," Owen conceded, his voice heavy with resignation. "We'll win in the end, we just need to bide our time."

As they approached the colliery, the sight of the familiar pithead brought no comfort. Instead, it served as a grim reminder of the harsh reality they would soon return to. The men shuffled towards their homes, their steps dragging and heads bowed low. The once burning determination now replaced with a cold acceptance of their fate.

"Right lads, Rhys and I are going to the hall to tell the gaffer we're going back to work and putting a stop to the evictions. And remember, we fought as hard as we could, just like the other proud men of these valleys. But this time, it wasn't enough."

"We may have to put up and shut up for now," added Rhys, "but it won't be forever."

Their voices faded into the evening as they trudged up the hill, dusk settling in around them.

"There's no denying it, Rhys. We can't keep this up. The lads are spent, and if we don't go back to Huntingdon's, we'll starve."

"Better the devil you know, eh?" Rhys replied, bitterness lacing his words. "But what kind of life is that, Da? Working ourselves to death for scraps?"

"Better than no life at all," Owen said quietly. "The other colliery owners, they're in open revolt. If we don't make some sort of peace, they'll crush us. Huntingdon's is bad, but he's not the worst of 'em."

"Seems we've got no choice then," Rhys sighed, the fight seeping out of him. "We'll go back, take what we can get. But it doesn't sit right with me, Da. Feels like we're giving in."

"Sometimes, lad, survival means swallowing your pride," Owen said, placing a firm hand on his son's shoulder. "We'll live to fight another day. And who knows? Maybe one day, things will change."

"Maybe," Rhys echoed, though his tone was far from hopeful.

The thought of returning to the pits under such dire terms was almost too much to bear. However, as he looked into his father's tired eyes, he knew they had no other option.

On their return, Owen and Rhys sat across from each other at their wood wormed dinner table, the weight of the day's events hanging heavily between them, with only one small candle to light the room and two thin bowls of soup that Sian dropped off to fill their bellies.

*

The heavy oak door to Huntington Manor creaked open, revealing Charles Huntington in his study. He leaned back in his leather chair, a rare smile gracing his lips as he discussed the Davies' news with Gerald Price.

"Finally," he muttered before puffing on a fat cigar. "The acrimony that had plagued our every waking moment for months is over."

Gerald Price nodded, trying to hide his disappointment.

*

The clinic bustled with activity as cuts were cleaned and dressed, bruises examined, and hot soup provided. While the men were able to return to work, the widows remained at risk, lacking funds to cover their accommodation and with no real right to stay if there were no coal men in their cottages.

Sian Williams locked herself in the consultation room at Ebba's insistence. She had been tirelessly liaising with employment agencies in Cardiff, Swansea, and Bristol. On her desk lay two piles—one with job opportunities, the other with widows' names. The unmarried ladies could easily find positions as live-in servants for the growing merchant classes in the industrial and commercial heartlands. However, those with children faced a harder challenge, often having to cram into shared living spaces or rely on staff accommodation.

As Gwen checked on their progress, Sian reported that she was unable to help about twenty of the widows.

Gwen suggested asking Mr Huntingdon for temporary housing until better solutions could be found, while Ebba looked into potential opportunities with the Salvation Army for cooking, cleaning, and laundry services.

> The miners gathered at the Working Men's Club, their faces bore shadowed scars from recent violent clashes against the black legs, who would now stand beside them to increase production. As they raised a glass together and toasted "to better days", their voices sounded tired yet hopeful.

The future remained uncertain, and challenges loomed ahead. But in their shared struggle, they found a flicker of resilience. As they bit their tongues and prepared to return to the pits once again, they carried with them both physical scars from their fight and the faintest glimmer of hope for a brighter future.

CHAPTER 30

The clatter of hobnailed boots rang through the valley as the miners trudged back to the colliery, their faces flat with resignation. Ebba watched from the clinic window, her heart heavy seeing their crushed bodies trudge along. The strike had ended but the tension lingered like a thick fog, threatening to suffocate any glimmer of hope. It was an uneasy peace with Huntingdon.

> "They're back at it then? It seems odd seeing them work and not picket," Sian commented, stepping up beside Ebba, her arms full of freshly laundered arm slings.

Ebba nodded, a sigh escaping her lips.

> "Yes, but at what cost? Their spirits are broken and their wages are the same, Sian."

As if on cue, a group of miners passed by, their voices rising in a chorus of jeers and taunts aimed at Huntingdon's carriage as it weaved its way to the colliery.

> "Bloody toff. Lining your pockets while we risk our lives!" one shouted, his fist raised in defiance.

Sian shook her head, her eyes glistening with unshed tears.

"It's not right. All this acrimony is poisoning the village. I don't want to raise little Gethin in such a bitter place!"

Ebba placed a comforting hand on Sian's shoulder.

"I know, Sian. We'll do everything we can to support them, even if it's just being a listening ear and providing a warm meal. Things will sort themselves out—eventually they always do."

Sian straightened her shoulders, newfound determination etched on her face.

"I better get these slings back in the store room."

As Sian hurried off, Ebba couldn't help but admire the young widow's resilience. Despite her own struggles, Sian had thrown herself into her work at the clinic and still did her shifts at the shop. She was becoming a wonderful nurse, her gentle touch and kind words bringing comfort to those in need. Ebba once asked her why she was such a relentless force, and she explained that when she didn't keep busy, she soon fell into melancholy.

A soft gurgle drew Ebba's attention to the corner of the room, where Elliot sat cradling little Gethin in his arms. The sight warmed her heart, and she couldn't help but smile at the adoring look on her husband's face as he cooed at the baby.

"Who's a handsome little lad, then?" Elliot murmured, tickling Gethin's chin and eliciting a delighted giggle. "Is it you? Is it? I bet it is."

As Ebba watched the tender moment unfold, she knew Elliot was going to be an incredible father. The way he doted on Gethin, his gentle patience showing through warmed her heart.

"Back soon, my love. Just off to the store room to help Sian."

*

Ebba didn't go to the storeroom; she went to the consultation room. Her hand drifted to her stomach, a subconscious gesture she found herself doing more often lately. The possibility of a new life growing inside her filled her with a mixture of excitement and trepidation. She desperately wanted to be a mother, to share the love and devotion she and Elliot had for each other with a child of their own. But the timing—it was oh so wrong.

She tried to listen with the stethoscope but it was pointless. Although she wasn't one for following the advice of wise women, she did have a metallic taste in her mouth, and her sense of smell was heightened. Was that another sign? She'd been off her food in the mornings, and Aunt Flo had not visited for some time which she attributed to the stress she'd been under. Her hands slid up and she felt her bosom. There was definitely new soreness, a tenderness that couldn't be denied. If she were honest, there was too much evidence to reach any other conclusion. The days of denial were finally over. The Chadwicks were going to be parents.

Through the crack of the door, Gwen spied on Ebba with a concerned look.

> *'Another secret to keep,'* she bemoaned to herself. *'I hate keeping secrets. My heart's always on my sleeve—until now.'*

Fortuitously, the midwife slipped away before she was discovered.

Conscious that she would soon be missed, Ebba returned to the main room in the clinic and glanced over at her husband who was now engrossed in a game of pat-a-cake with Gethin.

Elliot had been working tirelessly on his research paper and he looked exhausted most of the time. It was nice to see him enjoying himself, however briefly. She noticed his eyes were drooping as he looked down at Gethin, and it wasn't even noon yet.

That was when Ebba decided she would keep her news of impending motherhood to herself for a little while longer, at least until she was absolutely certain and Elliot had made more progress with his work. She couldn't bear the thought of distracting him from his mission, not when so much was at stake, and he was always such a fusspot when she needed help. Ebba thought about asking Gwen for her opinion but decided it wasn't fair to make her friend keep secrets.

The rest of the first day after the strike was relatively uneventful until a commotion outside drew Ebba's attention back to the window. Her eyes widened as she saw a procession of Salvation Army officers marching down the street, led by none other than William Booth himself. Beside him walked Jess and John Chadwick, flanked by cart boys hauling wagons full of supplies.

"Elliot, come and see this," Ebba called out, her voice tinged with awe.

Elliot joined her at the window, still cradling Gethin in his arms.

"By Jove, it's my parents! And is that—?"

As the group made their way towards the clinic, Ebba confirmed with excitement:

"William Booth? I can't believe it!"

She watched as they walked and noticed the air was filled with gratitude and relief, a balm to the wounded spirits of Cwmgryf. Elliot chimed in, his wry smile matching his joyous question.

"Are those new blankets?"

"Yes!" trilled Ebba with glee.

In the midst of it all, William Booth stepped forward and his clear, strong voice rang out above the heads of the crowd.

> "Brothers and sisters, we stand with you in your time of need. Let us remember the virtues that bind us together: temperance, compassion, and the unbreakable bonds of brotherhood. And in this spirit of togetherness, we bring donations that will make a difference to you brave men and women."

The crowd murmured in agreement, their faces turned towards the charismatic leader. Ebba felt proud as she watched Jess and John move among the people with kindness and strength. Ever since they had taken her in and raised her like their own child, she had wanted for nothing. And even now as a married woman, their generosity and compassion continued.

As Booth's speech drew to a close, the army brass band struck up a triumphant tune, lifting the spirits of all who heard it. Ebba leaned into Elliot's side for comfort.

> "It looks like we've weathered the storm, my love," she whispered.

> "Yes, I think we've come through the worst of it. I'm glad I sent a personal letter to William; it seems to have done the trick," Elliot replied with a wry smile.

He pressed a gentle kiss to her temple as Gethin wriggled between them.

> "Together, my darling," Ebba said with a grin. "We'll face whatever comes our way and cope with it together."

The trailblazing young doctor was so happy she felt like she could burst. Should she confess her condition? No, it wasn't the time.

> "Elliot! Ebba! You must show us around!" exclaimed John and Jess. "Your work here has inspired many other citadels, you have no idea."

Later that afternoon, as the music uplifted the community and brought them together in a rare moment of delight, Ebba allowed herself to believe that brighter days were ahead. For Cwmgryf, her loyal little team, Elliot, and the new life growing within her—there was a renewed promise of hope and brotherhood for times yet to come.

CHAPTER 31

As the Salvation Army's visit drew to a close, William Booth found himself surrounded by a throng of journalists eager to hear his thoughts on the miners' plight. He smiled warmly and with compassion as he began to speak.

> "The resilience and strength of the working class never cease to amaze me," Booth declared, his voice carrying across the gathered crowd in the hall. "These men and women toil tirelessly, risking their lives each day to provide for their families and fuel the engines of progress. Thanks to the work of the Chadwicks, there now exists a basic safety net here in the village whenever someone is in need. No one will be crushed by random misfortune again. This experiment, even in the darkest hours of the strike, has brought hope to this valley and may it continue."

The journalists scribbled furiously, trying to capture every word, as Booth—the great raconteur—captivated them. Then, ever the diplomat and good Christian, Booth acknowledged the challenges faced by colliery owners as well.

> "The changing economy presents difficulties for all; old industries fading away and new ones blossoming," he conceded, furrowing his brow in thought. "But together, with a strong spirit,

respect, determination, and flexibility, Britain will be on the path to true prosperity for all."

As the interview concluded, Booth shook hands with the journalists, his message of hope and solidarity resonating in the hearts of all who heard it.

In the village, a light shone from the Chadwicks' cottage. Elliot sat hunched over his desk, surrounded by a sea of papers and notes. There was no time to waste. The spotlight had been placed on Cwmgryf, and his white paper was more important than ever. Designing a workable yet cash-strapped and oversubscribed care provision system in the area had consumed every waking moment. As he prepared to present his findings to councils, benevolent trusts, and MPs, he felt a surge of nervous energy.

He reread his notes, his mind whirling with possibilities. The elderly, the sick, and the infirm—they were the ones who needed support the most, and they were going to get it without being sent to the workhouse. As he looked out the window at the crisp evening air, Elliot knew that his work had the potential to change lives. He was about to put his plan into action.

*

The Cardiff Town Hall meeting room was cramped, filled with council members, charity representatives, philanthropists, and government officials. Elliot took a deep breath, trying to steady his voice as he began his presentation.

"Ladies and gentlemen, I'm here today with a proposal that could change our community entirely," he said, scanning the room. "For too long, we've ignored our most vulnerable, leaving them to suffer in the workhouse. But what if we had a better system that actually helped people instead of locking them away? It sounds crazy, but my plan proves it's possible. Please turn to page seven in your pamphlets. Let's us begin."

He laid out his vision for a future where everyone's needs were met, regardless of their health.

"If we combine our resources and work together, we can create a caring system that supports everyone. Just like how smaller communities take care of each other, this will become the norm in twenty years," Elliot declared passionately. "We have a responsibility to the elderly, sick, and infirm—we cannot let them down."

As he answered questions and addressed concerns from the audience, Elliot felt more determined than ever. This wasn't just a white paper; it was a chance to make a real difference for industrialised and rural Britain.

And as the meeting drew to a close with promises of support from various individuals and organizations, Elliot knew there would be challenges ahead. But with the support of the philanthropic community and the guidance of his Salvation Army family, he was ready to tackle whatever obstacles stood in his way to make his bold plan a reality.

In Cwmgryf and beyond, news spread like wildfire about Booth's visit and Elliot's ambitious proposal. Excitement buzzed through the streets as miners and their families gathered in groups, hopeful for change after their recent strike.

> "Did you hear what Booth said?" one miner asked his friend with a spark in his eye. "He's speaking up for us, telling everyone about our struggles and how we deserve better conditions and healthcare. No one has ever done that before."

His companion nodded, a grin spreading across his face.

> "And Chadwick is working on a plan to make it happen. Can you imagine? Us funding our own care and taking care of our own! It could mean the end of the workhouse!"

As the discussions continued, Reverend Thomas Jenkins emerged from his chapel, observing the scene with keen eyes. He approached a group of women huddled together in conversation.

> "Ladies," he said, his gentle voice cutting through their discussion. "I couldn't help but overhear. It

seems that change is on the horizon for our little corner of the world."

One of the women, a widow with a faded shawl drawn tight around her shoulders, looked up at him with a mix of hope and trepidation.

"Do you really think it's possible, Reverend? After all we've been through, could things really get better?"

Reverend Jenkins laid a comforting hand on her shoulder, his eyes crinkling with a warm smile.

"My dear, with faith and determination, anything is possible. And from what I've seen, our little community has both in spades."

As the conversations continued, a sense of purpose began to take hold. Committees were formed, plans were made, and the people of Cwmgryf once again began to envision a future where their well-being was not just a dream, but a reality. Instead of working together to put an end to hardship, they were now united in creating a fresh new start.

Miles away in London, William Mabon sat in his parliamentary office with newspapers spread out before him. Booth's words leapt off the page as a clarion call for change that he knew he couldn't ignore.

He thought of the miners, their faces etched with sacrifice. He thought of the widows and children struggling to make ends meet in the wake of tragedy. And he knew, with a certainty that settled deep in his bones, that he had to take action.

Mabon began to draft his speech, his pen flying across the page as the words poured out of him. He vowed he would take Elliot's message to the floors of Westminster and, he would not rest until the people of Cwmgryf and people like them had the care and support they so desperately needed.

He reached out to fellow MPs and activists, like Keir Hardie and Dai o'r Nant, who both shared his beliefs in social justice. Together, they would form a united front that could not be ignored.

As the hours passed and the candles burned low, Mabon felt a sense of purpose unlike any before. This was more than mere politics; it was a chance to truly make a difference in the lives of those he served.

With a final flourish of his pen, he set down the speech and leaned back in his chair. A strong determination settled over him, ready for the long and difficult road ahead. But with his convictions and the support of his allies, he would not be deterred.

CHAPTER 32

The air hung heavy with anticipation as the miners representatives gathered in the dimly lit union office. Ebba Chadwick stood at the front of the room, her eyes scanning the sea of weathered faces before her. She could feel the weight of their hopes and fears, the desperation that had driven them to this moment.

> "Thank you all for coming," she began, her voice steady despite the nerves fluttering in her stomach. "I know that many of you have been through unspeakable hardships, that you've seen your friends and loved ones suffer in ways that no one should ever have to endure."

A murmur of agreement rippled through the crowd, and Ebba saw heads nodding in recognition. She took a deep breath and continued:

> "But today, we have a chance to change that. Today, we begin the fight for a better future. My husband's plan, together with funds from The Salvation Army, the Miner's Benevolent Trust, and a mystery donor I am yet to identify, means the pilot scheme here has been a success. We wish to build on that success."

Beside her, Owen Davies stepped forward, his broad shoulders squared with determination.

"We've all seen the toll that these harsh working conditions, poor safety, poor sanitation, long hours, slow modernisation, have taken on our community," he said, his Welsh lilt filling the room. "The accidents, the injuries, the lives cut short by disease and despair. It's time for us to stand up and say enough is enough."

As Owen spoke, Rhys moved through the crowd, distributing sheets of paper and pens.

"We need your stories," he explained, his voice low and urgent. "Your experiences, your struggles. We need to show the world what's really happening here in Cwmgryf. We have parliamentary interest in this proposal and we must seize this opportunity for all we are worth."

Sian watched as the miners began to write, their hands shaking with emotion as they poured out their hearts onto the page. The more educated ones who finished first helped the slower writers and the illiterate share their opinions. She felt a lump rising in her throat as she thought of her own story, of the husband she had lost and the child she now cared for. If Ebba, Mrs Morgan, Gwen and Rhys had not stood by her, she would be alone and melancholic in the Rhondda Workhouse!

As the meeting drew to a close, Reverend Jenkins stepped forward, his face lined with compassion.

Let us pray," he said, his voice a soothing balm in the charged atmosphere. "Let us ask for strength

and guidance as we embark on this journey, and
let us remember that we are all children of God,
deserving of love and respect."

The workers bowed their heads as the Reverend spoke, their hearts lifted by his words of comfort and support. And as they filed out of the union office, Ebba felt a sense of pride and purpose swelling within her.

"Tell your men and women folk to bring us their
letters we are collecting them for a week. Please!
Impress upon them how urgent this is. It's our
one big chance! Seize it gentlemen!"

'This is just the beginning', she thought, her mind already racing with plans for the letter-writing campaign and the delegation to Parliament. *'We will not rest until justice is done.'*

As the days passed, the community mobilised with a fervour that Ebba had never seen before. Letters poured out to local newspapers and Members of Parliament, each one a heartfelt plea for change and support. And as the evidence of workplace accidents and health issues mounted, brought out into the open, not logged in dusty ledgers, the case for action grew stronger with each passing day.

And as the delegation to Parliament began to take shape, Ebba felt a sense of nervous excitement building within her. She knew that the road ahead would be difficult, that they would face opposition and scepticism at every turn. But she also knew that they had the truth on their side, and the unshakeable conviction that comes from fighting for what is right.

We will make them listen, she vowed, her eyes blazing with determination. We will make them see the injustice that has been done, and we will not rest until change is made.

And so, with hearts full of hope and minds steeled with resolve, the community of Cwmgryf prepared to take their fight to the highest halls of power, ready to stand up for their rights and demand a better future for all.

CHAPTER 33

The rhythmic chugging of the train filled the air as it carried the delegation from the village to London. Owen Davies sat beside Elliot, his weathered hands clasped tightly around a briefcase stuffed full with first-hand accounts from the men and women of South Wales.

"Never thought I'd see the day," he murmured, his eyes fixed on the passing landscape. "Miners from Cwmgryf, heading to Parliament to speak our truth."

Elliot nodded, his own nerves thrumming beneath his skin.

"It's certainly different than standing on a stool at the Working Men's Club! It's a momentous occasion, Owen. We're making history today. I am honoured to have you by my side. We've made quite a team over these past few months."

On the other side of the aisle, Reverend Jenkins and respected philanthropist Lord Marlborough were deep in conversation, their heads bent together. Ebba watched them for a moment, amazed at the unlikely friendship between the humble pastor and wealthy lord.

As the train arrived at London's Paddington Station, the delegation gathered their belongings and stepped out onto the bustling platform. A sea of faces greeted them—delegates from all over the country, united in support. Banners and signs bobbed above the crowd, with slogans like 'Fair Wages for Honest Work' and 'Safety First in the Workplace.'

Elliot felt a swell of emotion as he took in the scene. This is what solidarity looks like, he thought proudly. This is what it means to stand together.

As they made their way through the busy streets, the Cwmgryf delegation joined forces with other activist groups, exchanging greetings and words of encouragement. The air was charged with energy, a fierce determination that could be felt by all.

> "We're not alone in this fight," Owen exclaimed, his voice filled with emotion. "Just look at all these people—from different walks of life—coming together for change. And we can achieve it with our minds and hearts, not violence."

*

In the gallery above, Ebba and Elliot sat with the rest of the delegation, their hearts pounding as they watched Mabon make his case to the House. Owen leaned forward, his eyes fixed on the MP, hanging on every word.

> "The evidence is clear," Mabon continued, holding up a thick sheaf of papers. "Workplace accidents, wage disparities, health issues—all of these problems are rampant in the mines of Cwmgryf and others across the country. This nation is built

on their toil and it is time to recognise the workers of our fair nation for their contribution to the economic power house that is Britain and her Empire."

Ebba felt a surge of pride and the prickle of tears welling up as she watched Mabon speak, his words giving weight and credibility to the struggles of her community. *'He's doing it! He's actually making them listen.'*

Around the chamber, the reactions of the MPs varied. Some from the industrial heartlands nodded in sympathy, their faces etched with concern. Others looked sceptical, their arms crossed and their mouths set in thin lines. And still, others appeared openly hostile, their eyes narrowing as they listened to Mabon's impassioned speech, tutting, shaking their heads and adjusting pure gold cufflinks, staring at solid silver pocket watches to emphasise they had somewhere better to be.

But even as the opposition mounted, Ebba could see the tide beginning to turn. Journalists sat beside them scribbled furiously in their notebooks, their pens flying across the pages as they captured every word. How Ebba wished she could read shorthand.

She knew that the papers would play a crucial role in amplifying the voices of the workers, in shaping public opinion and putting pressure on those in power. With pamphleteers and working class newspapers gaining a bigger circulation every year, coordinating the campaign was becoming easier by the year.

As Mabon concluded his speech, the chamber erupted in a mixture of applause and jeers. The delegation from Cwmgryf rose to their feet, their faces beaming with pride and gratitude.

It had gone well. But would it be enough?

*

In the days and weeks that followed, the impact of Mabon's speech and the media coverage began to ripple across the nation. Newspapers splashed the story across their front pages, their bold headlines proclaiming the plight of heavy industry workers and the urgent need for change. Letters poured into the offices of many Members of Parliament, their impoverished constituents demanding action and expressing their outrage at the conditions endured by the working class.

On the streets of London, Cardiff, Clydebank, Liverpool, Leeds, Bradford, Burnley and beyond, people gathered in pubs, in marketplaces, and on street corners, their voices rising in heated debate. Had Cwmgryf proven that the workhouse was outdated and the parish funding and tyranny of Workhouse Guardians and cruel masters could come to an end!

Others, however, remained indifferent or even hostile to the cause. They dismissed the working class struggles as the inevitable consequence of progress, arguing that the march of industry demanded sacrifices from all.

But even amidst the opposition, the tide of public opinion was slowly beginning to shift. The sheer weight of the evidence presented by Mabon, the raw emotion of their testimony, was impossible to ignore. Slowly but surely, thanks to the newspapers, more and more people began to see the injustice of the current system, and the urgent need for reform.

Exhausted when they got back, Elliot retired immediately but Ebba took a moment to sit beside the small range in her cottage, and as she settled, she felt a wonderous flicker in her belly. The secret joy that she had not yet shared with Elliot was most definitely true.

She placed a hand on her stomach, imagining the life growing inside her, the future that they were fighting for. *'This is for you'*, she whispered, her eyes filled with determination. *'This is for all of us.'*

Now all she had to consider was when to tell Elliot. With the parliamentary presentation complete, there was no need to wait much longer.

CHAPTER 34

Alas, Ebba didn't get her chance to reveal her secret and it felt like the right time would never appear before the birth! It was one thing after another, much to her chagrin. Worse, Elliot, ever devoted to his cause, had been drawn even deeper into committee meetings and trust gatherings, each one seemingly more urgent than the last. Their time together had dwindled to fleeting moments.

Ebba yearned to share her news with him, but something held her back—perhaps it was the weight of his responsibilities or her own stubborn resolve to continue her work unimpeded. He would surely tell her to rest and keep her distance from those with contagious diseases. As time passed, the uneasy deceit became easier to bear.

*

Cardiff's Freemasons' Hall loomed ahead with its stout building and Greek-style Palladian portico as one of Cwmgryfs' residents approached. Henry Blackwood, retired yet never idle, sat at a table with his spectacles perched on the bridge of his nose as he scanned a map laid out before him.

"Charles, if you will," Blackwood began, gesturing towards a section of the map. "I've been pondering over the geology of this and I believe we may have overlooked something crucial."

Huntingdon leaned in, his eyes narrowing in concentration.

"Go on—"

"I've been revisiting the old colliery surveys and there's an anomaly near the western ridge that I believe warrants a second look."

Charles Huntingdon leaned over the map, a glint of amusement in his eye.

"This is a missed opportunity, no doubt about it. The survey technology back then was rudimentary. But now, I'm convinced there's a substantial seam we overlooked, hidden beneath that ridge."

Blackwood leaned forward, his voice a low whisper.

"This could be the salvation of Cwmgryf Colliery, Charles. Don't you want to know for sure?"

Charles let out an approving murmur, his face brightening with a newfound hope that had been missing for far too long.

"That is nothing short of miraculous, Henry. If this works, it could change everything for the colliery—and for Cwmgryf."

"Indeed," Blackwood replied, his tone measured but hopeful.

The next day, Huntingdon had some of his men doing some exploratory boring to see if Blackwood's idea had merit.

The news of the potential rich seam had spread like wildfire through the village. For months, the community had been grappling with uncertainty—miners working gruelling hours for dwindling returns, families struggling to make ends meet, Charles Huntingdon battling with an increasingly unprofitable mine. But now, there was a glimmer of hope, a chance that the colliery might prosper once more.

*

"Ebba, there you are!" Gwen's voice cut through Ebba's thoughts.

The midwife approached, her keen eyes narrowing slightly as they took in Ebba's appearance.

"Morning, Gwen," Ebba greeted her friend, feeling a pang of guilt.

She knew Gwen's sharp midwife mind wouldn't miss the subtle changes in her.

"How are you faring today?" Gwen asked, her tone casual but laced with concern. "You look a bit peaky, if you don't mind me saying."

Ebba chuckled softly.

"Just tired, I suppose. It's been a busy few weeks."

"Busy, indeed." Gwen's gaze lingered on Ebba's face, then drifted lower, taking in the slight swell beneath her dress. "You've been working yourself too hard."

"There's always work to be done," Ebba replied, avoiding Gwen's penetrating stare. "And with Elliot so tied up with meetings, someone has to keep things running."

"True enough," Gwen conceded, though her expression remained thoughtful. "But you mustn't forget to take care of yourself, Ebba. You're no good to anyone if you run yourself into the ground."

"Don't worry about me," Ebba said, forcing a lightness into her voice that she didn't quite feel. "I'm stronger than I look."

"That you are," Gwen agreed. But her eyes spoke volumes.

She had seen the way Ebba's hands trembled ever so slightly and how she seemed to tire more quickly these days. There were other signs too—subtle shifts in posture and the way Ebba would sometimes pause and press a hand to her lower back.

"Let's go for a walk," Gwen suggested, linking her arm through Ebba's. "A bit of fresh air will do us both good."

They strolled along the footpath that wound along the perimeter of the village the village, surrounded by the sounds of everyday life—children's laughter, the clatter of pots from open windows, the rhythmic clang of the blacksmith's hammer, and the clank of the colliery. Noisy—but normal.

"Have you heard about the new seam?" Gwen asked, breaking the comfortable silence between them.

"Yes, it's all anyone can talk about," Ebba replied.

"Aye, it's a blessing if it proves true. But we can't count our chickens before they hatch."

As they walked, Gwen's mind raced. She couldn't shake the feeling that something more was at play with Ebba. Years of midwifery had honed her observational skills; she knew the signs of pregnancy when she saw them. But why would Ebba keep such a thing secret for so long?

The question gnawed at her, mingling with her worry for her friend's well-being.

"Ebba," Gwen began gently, stopping to face her. "If there's ever anything you need to talk about, you know I'm here for you, don't you?"

For a moment, Ebba's façade wavered, her eyes betraying a flicker of vulnerability. But she quickly composed herself, offering Gwen a reassuring smile.

"I know, Gwen. Thank you."

As they continued their walk, Gwen silently vowed to keep a close watch on Ebba, determined to support her friend through whatever trials lay ahead.

*

Ebba leaned heavily against the clinic's worn wooden table, her face ashen beneath the soft glow of the gas lamp. Her fingers trembled as she tried to grip the edge for support, but a wave of dizziness swept over her, forcing her to sink into the nearest chair.

"Ebba!" Gwen's voice was a mix of concern and authority as she rushed to her friend's side. "You look dreadful. Sit still for a moment, will you?"

"Just a bit tired, that's all," Ebba said, managing a weak smile.

"Rubbish," Gwen retorted with a valley lilt, softening the firmness of her words.

She knelt beside Ebba, her experienced eyes scanning every inch of her friend's pallid face.

"This is more than just fatigue. I've seen this before, and you know it."

Ebba closed her eyes, feeling tears pricking at the edges. She had hoped to maintain her secret a little longer, but Gwen's persistence was unwavering. The walls of her resolve began to crumble.

"Please," Gwen whispered, her hand gently squeezing Ebba's. "Tell me what's going on. I think I can guess."

The room seemed to close in around Ebba. A sob escaped her lips, and she covered her face with trembling hands.

"Yes," she admitted through her tears. "I'm pregnant."

Gwen's heart clenched. There it was. The cathartic confession.

"Oh, Ebba," she murmured, wrapping an arm around her and her soul in a little white lie. "Why didn't you say anything sooner? You know I'm here to help you—as a professional and a friend."

"Because—" Ebba's voice broke, and she took a shuddering breath. "Because I don't want to distract Elliot. I wanted him to be the first to know. But he has so much on his shoulders already. And— and I can't stop working, Gwen. This village needs us. I'll hardly be the first working mother in Britain."

"Ebba, you need to think about your health and the baby's," Gwen insisted gently but firmly. "Elliot deserves to know. Why shouldn't he be involved as soon as possible? You've seen how he dotes on little Gethin. He loves you and will want to help."

"Help?" Ebba's laugh was laced with frustration. "I can see it now—him fussing over me, telling me to rest, take it easy. Have another cup of tea. Put your feet up. He'll have me wrapped up in more cotton wool than a patient after a wisdom tooth extraction. But who will tend to the sick? Who will care for the injured miners when they come stumbling in? I can't afford to stop, Gwen. Not now that we can prove this system is working, not with the eyes of the press and Westminster on us."

Gwen looked into Ebba's eyes and saw fierce determination mixed with fear and doubt. She sighed deeply, torn between her duty as a midwife and her loyalty to her friend.

"Alright," Gwen said slowly, her words heavy with resignation. "But promise me one thing—if it gets too much, if you feel unwell or if there's any sign of trouble, you must tell me immediately. No secrets, understood?"

"Understood."

A few weeks later, as Ebba got changed for bed, Elliot noticed her growing bump and teased her.

"You'll have to cut down on all the Welsh cakes the women-folk keep giving you."

"Er, yes," Ebba replied mischievously as she turned to bury herself under their sheets and hide.

CHAPTER 35

The sky above Cwmgryf was a sullen grey. A soft drizzle began to fall, soaking into the cobblestones and turning the lanes into a slick, treacherous path. On their way to the Working Men's Club, Owen Davies pulled his cap lower over his brow. Beside him, Rhys walked with purposeful strides, his hair glistening with tiny water droplets.

> "Blasted rain," muttered Rhys. "It's been days since we last saw the sun."

As they passed by Mrs Morgan's shop, the murmur of a conversation caught their ears. Gwen Price's voice, usually so warm and comforting, now held a sharp edge.

> "Edith, I'm at my wit's end," Gwen said, her voice shaking with barely suppressed anger. "Gerald has been harassing Mary again. He cornered her down by the lane, threatening to put her out on the streets if she doesn't—you know—"

> "Comply?"

Gwen nodded grimly.

> "You know what that snake of a cousin is like when it comes to women he thinks can't fight back. No woman is safe."

"That man's a menace," Rhys hissed, his voice low but still seething.

"Let's find him," Owen said, his tone steely.

"Now."

They moved away from the shop, their pace quickening towards the club house—normally a dimly lit haven for men seeking solace in drink after a hard day's labour. Tonight, it would be the venue for a showdown.

Pushing through the swinging double doors, Owen and Rhys were met with the stale stench of ale and eye-stinging cigarette smoke. The low hum of conversation filled the room, but it was Gerald's voice that cut through the din—loud and laced with arrogance.

> "I told her she'll do what I tell 'er to do, or I'll make sure she regrets it," Gerald boasted, leaning back in his chair with a smug grin plastered across his face.

Bryn Jones, sitting opposite him, grunted in agreement, lifting his mug in a crude toast.

> "Cheers to that," Bryn said, slurring his words from drink.

Owen and Rhys exchanged a glance, their determination hardening. They moved through the crowd, their presence drawing curious looks from other patrons. Reaching Gerald's table, they stood tall, casting shadows over the man who had brought so much misery to their community.

"Evening," Owen's voice was calm, but there was an unmistakable edge to it.

Gerald looked up, his smile faltering for just a moment before he regained his composure.

"Ah, the Davies boys," he drawled, leaning back in his chair with a look of feigned indifference. "To what do I owe this pleasure?"

"Enough of your games," Rhys cut in, his fists clenching at his sides. "Stay away from Mary. Stay away from Sian. In fact, stay away from all the women in this village."

"Or what?" Gerald sneered, his eyes glinting with malice.

Bryn, slumped beside him, let out a coarse laugh.

"Yeah, these two are pathetic," he slurred while again raising his mug unsteadily. "Just like that laughable strike of theirs."

"Shut yer mouth, Bryn," Rhys snapped, losing his temper. "This has nothing to do with you."

"Calm down lads," the landlord called from behind the bar, sounding weary. "Take it outside if yer must."

"Listen to him," Gerald mocked, taking a leisurely sip of his drink. "You don't want to cause a scene now, do you?"

"You're the one causing scenes," Owen shot back, his voice low but filled with menace. "Preying on women, using your position to intimidate them. It ends now."

"Is that so?" Gerald taunted, slowly standing up. He was a few inches shorter than Owen, but his arrogance made up for the difference.

"And how do you plan to stop me? More righteous speeches until I fall into an deep slumber?"

"Don't underestimate us," Rhys warned, stepping closer with tense muscles, ready for the impending fight. "We won't stand by and let you abuse our women like this."

"Big words from a boy," Gerald sneered, his gaze flickering with contempt. "But that's all they are—just words."

"I've had enough!" the landlord barked, losing his patience. "I won't have my place turned into a battleground. If you have issues, settle them elsewhere."

"Fine by me," Gerald said with a lazy grin, turning his back on them. "I've had enough of this drivel anyway. Let's finish off that drink you've got, Bryn."

"Good idea!"

"Mark my words, Price," Owen called after him, his voice thunderous. "This isn't over."

"Not by a long shot," Rhys added, his eyes burning with unspoken promises.

As Gerald sauntered towards the door, Bryn stumbled after him, still chuckling to himself. The tension in the room crackled like static, leaving everyone in uneasy silence and the furious father and son to finish their pints.

CHAPTER 36

"Right, let's go," Owen muttered to Rhys as they exchanged a determined look.

The drizzle evaporated against their hot, angry faces as they stepped out into the night.

"He's not getting away with it," Rhys vowed quietly as they took up their vigil once more.

"Absolutely not," added Owen.

The club door swung shut behind them, sealing their promise in the damp, heavy air. The streets were deserted, the usual bustle of Cwmgryf subdued by the wet weather. As they reached Bryn's cottage, Rhys and Owen stood together like sentinels against the darkness, united in their solidarity despite the chill and the challenges that lay ahead.

*

The drizzle had ceased, leaving the cobblestones slick and glistening. The cold night air cut through their thin jackets, but their simmering anger kept them warm.

"He's taking his time," Rhys muttered, shifting from one foot to the other.

"Patience, lad," Owen replied, his voice a low rumble. "He'll show soon enough."

Time dragged on until finally, Gerald staggered out of Bryn's front door and landed flat on the floor. As he struggled to his feet, Bryn and Price's laughter echoed down the empty lane.

"Get yerself up and get yerself home, yer great apeth," Bryn said before closing the door.

Gerald turned the corner and wobbled homeward.

"Now," Owen whispered, his eyes narrowing with purpose. They moved swiftly. The surprise was evident in Gerald's eyes when he saw them, but soon all he could see was stars.

Owen's fist connected with Gerald's jaw, sending him sprawling to the ground. The sickening sound of flesh meeting bone was oddly satisfying to the two men standing over him.

"Stay away from Mary," Owen commanded, kicking Gerald in the belly with every syllable.

"Or else," Rhys added, delivering a flurry of swift kicks to Gerald's lower back.

"Please, no more," Gerald wheezed, curled up in a defensive ball, his arrogance dissolving into fear as he realised the gravity of the situation.

"Remember this," Owen said, leaning down so his face was inches from Gerald's. "This is what happens when you prey on our women."

With one final punch to the head from Rhys, Gerald would think twice before crossing them or their women-folk again. They left him there lying battered, bloodied, and broken on the cobblestones, groaning in pain.

"Let's go," Owen said, straightening up. "Our message is clear."

As they walked away, the adrenaline began to ebb, leaving them with a grim satisfaction, then guilt. They had defended Mary's honour, but at what cost?

They had become thugs, no better than Price. By the time they got home, the weight of their actions settled heavily upon their consciences.

*

The next morning, Mrs Morgan peered out her shop window and saw Gerald walk past with a shiner and a cut on his cheek. His head hung low in shame.

'I must ask Ebba and Gwen about their investigation,' she thought to herself. *'Clearly, Gerald has been tormenting someone's friend or relative again.'*

"These women need our help, and fast," Edith said as she sipped her hot sweet tea.

"We all know what Gerald's up to, but no one will speak alone for fear of retribution—or the shame of being called a liar or a loose woman in court," added Gwen.

"I'll make a point of going round today while his face is still bruised. It will help prove we're serious about doing something," suggested Ebba.

"I can tell anyone who comes into the shop to expect your call," Mrs Morgan chimed in.

"Let's gather as much evidence as we can, and tomorrow I'll ask Elliot and Reverend Jenkins to personally hand it in at the police station. If the men hand it in, it's more likely to be believed and acted upon," said Gwen.

"Let's hope so, ladies. He's been playing this game for years and getting off scot-free," Ebba lamented.

The women Gwen visited that evening were hesitant at first, just like Ebba predicted. They feared for their safety if Gerald found out they had spoken against him. His evil tentacles had a habit of wrapping around anything he wanted to quash.

"Together, we are strong. The men can hand in our anonymous letters. And if the police question him when he has the black eye, they will know he's up to no good."

Ebba and Gwen quickly got to work gathering evidence and witness statements from the abused women. They collected torn clothing as proof of Gerald's violence, and Ebba made a doctor's report of any fresh bruising.

In the morning, Elliot dropped off a thick dossier of information at the station, and two hours later Mrs Morgan said she saw Price being walked in handcuffs to the station. After that, no one knew what happened to him.

*

Later that night, as they indexed and collated the evidence, Ebba sat by the fireplace. The warmth barely reached her bones against the cold of the old stone walls. She stared into the dancing flames, lost in thought. Nearby, Gwen and Sian shared a rare moment of quiet amidst the chaos of their lives.

> "How do you do it, Gwen?" Ebba suddenly asked, breaking the silence. "I feel like I'm being pulled in every direction and I can't keep up. As if I wasn't busy enough, now we have this Price situation to deal with."

Gwen looked up, her kind eyes reflecting understanding.

> "It's never easy, Ebba. We all struggle. But you're doing more than most. You're a doctor fighting for a cause you believe in, and soon to be a mother. It's a lot for anyone."

> "A mother!" Sian piped up as Ebba gave Gwen a dagger look for telling someone else her secret.

"Sorry, Ebba."

"Both of you, just make sure my Elliot doesn't find out. He's so close to being finished with all those research reports. I mean it! I hate keeping secrets, but it's for the best. For everyone."

"Gwen's right. We're all stretched thin, especially now with the threat of this flu epidemic. Just remember how much you've done for this community and all the others like it. You can't do it alone. You need to rely on Elliot and his network of activists to keep pushing ahead. You need to rest."

"That's just it," Ebba sighed, frustration lacing her voice. "I can't rest. Not when there's still so much to do."

"Lean on us," Sian said softly. "We're here for you, just as you've been here for us."

"Thank you," Ebba whispered, her heart heavy yet touched by their support. "I just hope I can find a way to manage it all."

"One step at a time," Gwen reassured her, reaching out to squeeze her hand.

A knock at the door interrupted their conversation. Gwen rose to answer it, revealing a young boy with flushed cheeks and fear in his wide eyes.

"Dr Chadwick, ma'am," he panted. "Me Da's taken ill. He's burning up and coughing something fierce."

"Flu?" Ebba asked, rising swiftly.

"Sounds like it," said Gwen. "It will rip through the valley like wildfire now."

"One last case and I'll rest. You can make me some soup if you want to be useful."

*

Ebba arrived at the modest cottage, its windows dark save for a single flickering candle. The boy's father lay on a makeshift bed in the corner, his face pale and slick with sweat, his breathing laboured.

"Mr Berry, it's Dr Chadwick," Ebba said softly, kneeling beside her patient.

The man was delirious and barely responding.

"Try and keep him cool, Billy—it is Billy, isn't it? If he gets cold and clammy, cover him up with a blanket. And make sure he has plenty of water. Thin soup would be good too. If his breathing gets worse, come and find us. We can get him some oil of camphor in hot water to inhale—clean his tubes out a bit. Does he suffer from black lung?"

Billy nodded, looking concerned. As they left the cottage, Sian asked with worry lacing her voice:

"That means every resident in this block of cottages has succumbed to the flu. Forty people?"

"It's a lot of cases—a lot of suffering," Gwen replied quietly. "But we'll manage somehow."

*

"Ebba, Gwen, over here!" Elliot's voice called from a corner of the room. He was bent over a miner whose laboured breaths echoed painfully in the small space.

"How is he?" Ebba asked, kneeling beside him.

"Not good," Elliot replied, his jaw set in grim determination. "We need more medicine, but the supplies are running low."

"Then we'll find a way," Ebba said firmly, though a wave of dizziness threatened to topple her.

She steadied herself against the edge of the cot, unwilling to show any sign of weakness.

"Ebba, you must rest," Elliot insisted, his eyes locking onto hers with unspoken concern.

"Later," she promised, knowing full well that 'later' might never come if they didn't act now.

As the day wore on, the clinic became a beacon of hope and desperation. Sian arrived, bringing bowls of steaming broth that offered some solace to the sick.

Rhys and Owen appeared next, their faces lined with exhaustion but their spirits undeterred.

"Did you see in the paper about Gerald?" Rhys quizzed,

"No. What did it say?"

"Take a look," Rhys said, pulling out a torn and crumpled newspaper clipping from his coat pocket.

"Cwmgryf:- Colliery foreman Gerald Price is to stand trial accused of tampering with official weighing scales to under weigh hewers' coal sacks, and serious assaults on widowed colliery tenants. Evidence strongly suggests guilt and the community awaits justice being served. If convicted, Evans faces a likely sentence of several years in prison."

"How's the seam coming along?" Ebba asked during a brief lull as Owen and Rhys wrestled with their consciences

"Slowly," Owen admitted, wiping sweat from his brow. "The men are pushing themselves hard, but this flu—"

He trailed off, shaking his head.

"We'll get through it," Rhys added, though his eyes betrayed the uncertainty he felt. "We always do."

The hours slipped by in a blur of activity and fatigue. As night fell, the chill deepened, seeping into bones already weary from endless toil. Ebba found herself standing by the window, gazing out at the darkened village. Lights flickered in the cottages, a fragile defiance against the encroaching darkness.

"Ebba." Elliot's voice was soft, almost a whisper. "You need to sleep."

"Just a little longer," she replied, not turning away from the window. "They need me."

"And I need you," he said, stepping closer, his hand resting gently on her shoulder. "We all do."

Ebba finally looked at him, seeing the same exhaustion mirrored in his eyes.

"We'll make it," she said, more for herself than for him.

From the street outside, the sound of coughing and murmured conversations drifted up, mingling with the distant clatter of mining equipment still at work. The dual challenges loomed large over Cwmgryf, casting a shadow of uncertainty over the future. Yet, within the clinic's walls, there was a sense of quiet resolve—a determination to face whatever came next with courage and solidarity.

"Let's go home," Elliot whispered, his voice gentle yet insistent.

"Alright," Ebba conceded, feeling the weight of the day settle upon her.

Together, they stepped out into the night, the path ahead uncertain but shared.

"Really, Elliot, it's just a cold," Ebba said, trying to convince both him and herself. "I'll be fine."

"Fine or not, you're pushing yourself too hard," he argued gently. "Please, let Gwen and me handle things for a while."

"Alright," she whispered, finally allowing herself to lean into his embrace. "But just for a little while. I'll have a lie down back at the cottage?"

"Happy?"

"Yes!" The trio chorused.

"Let's get you home," Elliot said softly, wrapping her arm over his shoulders for extra support. "Let's get you in your nightgown. You'll be less tempted to come back then!", Elliot chided playfully.

"Elliot, promise me you'll keep up with the research. It's important."

"Only if you promise to rest," he countered, buttoning up her nightgown. "Look, this barely does up. Have you been eating more Welsh cakes?"

"Yes," mumbled Ebba as her head lolled, before she fell into bed and was asleep within minutes.

It would be days before she regained proper consciousness, her body completely shutting down in a bid to survive.

CHAPTER 37

As Elliot entered their once happy and welcoming bedroom, he was struck by the eerie quietness. The only sound was his wife's laboured breathing as she lay motionless on the bed, propped up with his and her pillows. Her once vibrant features now pale and sunken from fever.

Gwen sat beside her friend, holding her hand and trying to distract her from her perilous condition with aimless chatter. But as soon as she stopped talking, Gwen's thoughts were consumed by gloom.

Elliot avoided staying in the bedroom for too long, preferring to focus on his work downstairs in the front room. He asked Gwen how Ebba was doing, wanting to know if there had been any change.

Gwen met his gaze with concern in her eyes.

"She's fighting, Elliot."

"Good," he replied, relieved. "But wait—what do you mean?"

"The thing is," Gwen hesitated before revealing a secret that Ebba had sworn her to keep. "She's pregnant—about twelve weeks along. She didn't want you worrying and fussing over her, so she made me promise not to tell you until now."

"Oh Ebba," Elliot said, stroking her hand gently. "I wish I could talk to you right now. That report can wait—you are more important to me than anything else."

"The baby seems fine for now and Ebba's fever has lessened slightly since she passed out earlier," Gwen continued. "But we need to focus on keeping them both safe until she recovers."

Elliot nodded, puzzled, trying to fathom the implications of the wave of information. He sank into an armchair by the bed, burying his head in his hands for a moment before pulling himself together.

Then he sat on the bed opposite Gwen, taking Ebba's hand and kissing it softly.

"You're going to get through this, my love," he whispered, his voice trembling.

"You'll be the most amazing mother to our child. You've fought through so much already in your life. Since you took your first breath. You can do this. Keep fighting, my love."

*

Days passed, with Ebba unconscious.

Sian and Gwen took turns checking on her. Elliot sat by her side, unable to sleep. He never left, holding her hand as if it could keep her in this world. Sometimes he placed his hand on her stomach, hoping for a sign of the bairn, but felt nothing.

Ebba's body fought hard but her long hours before falling ill, stress from the strike and pregnancy had taken a toll. The air grew stale in the small room, heavy with medicine and unspoken fears. He moistened her lips and spooned water into her mouth when she stirred.

On the fourth day, while Sian watched over her, Ebba woke up disorientated, dehydrated and demoralised—but alive.

*

Gwen felt pulled from pillar to post. The clinic was overflowing with vulnerable patients, all fighting off the flu. Her uncle was now bedridden and had to be positioned on the bed pan, which frustrated and embarrassed him. This was also a cause for concern for Gwen when she couldn't make it there. There were vigils for Ebba as well. It was bittersweet to receive a letter from Llewelyn telling her to expect him soon. Her wedding, something she had been looking forward to, was now on hold. She wondered why Llewelyn was even coming back, since he was hardly there now that the new coal seam was producing plenty of coal to be shipped to London.

As Elliot prepared to swap places with Gwen, there was a knock at the bedroom door.

"I came as soon as I heard," Llewellyn said. "Ifan told me about poor Ebba."

His gaze drifted to Ebba's lifeless form, propped up on pillows with her head lolling. He swallowed hard.

"How is she?"

"She's stirred a little bit more today, but she's not come round," Elliot replied in a croaking voice from exhaustion and worry.

Llewellyn nodded, his attention shifting to where Gwen sat, her head bowed in silent prayer.

"Gwen," he called softly. His voice was tender and full of love and devotion. "I had to come and see you. Did you get my letter?"

Gwen felt tears prick at the corners of her eyes as she saw the sincerity in Llewellyn's gaze.

"Can I talk to you alone? Do you mind, Elliot?"

"Please. There's not much we can do here apart from keeping Ebba company. You go ahead, Gwen. I'll see you tomorrow."

Elliot watched their faces fall when they thought he couldn't see them anymore.

*

Back at Uncle Ifan's cottage, Gwen wasn't in the mood to talk, but Llewellyn wasn't taking no for an answer.

"Hear me out, Gwen. The mine is secure now that the new seam is producing plenty of coal. That means my job is safe, as is yours. When I found out poor Ebba was struck down in the prime of life, it made me realize that none of us know how long our lives will be. We can't waste a single moment."

He took a deep breath and his next words tumbled out in a rush.

"Marry me, Gwen. Let's not wait any longer. I can get a certificate on my next sailing?"

Gwen's heart swelled with emotion and she leaned forward, pressing her forehead against his.

"Yes," she whispered, tears now flowing freely down her cheeks. "Yes, I'll marry you Llewellyn-- my childhood sweetheart, my rock, my soulmate. I'll ask Sian to sit with Ebba. Let's go see Reverend Jenkins tomorrow."

As Gwen and Llewellyn held hands, imagining a bright new future together, Elliot held Ebba's hand and his heart ached with each ragged breath she took.

*

The door opened one more time that evening. Sian crept in carrying a sleeping little Gethin in her arms. His cherubic face uplifted Elliot but also stabbed at his heart like a knife.

As she sat on the bed, the little boy awakened.

"I thought you might like some company," Sian said softly, placing the squirming baby in Elliot's arms before he could say no.

He cradled the boy close, tears slipping down his cheeks as Gethin cooed and reached for his face with his tiny pinkish fingers.

"Did you know your Aunty Ebba is a real fighter, just like you were when you were born a few weeks early?" he whispered, his voice choked with emotion. "She'll come back to us and she'll be playing hopscotch with you as soon as you can hop."

"I'm sorry, Sian. Could you take him back? I—please, just—it's too much."

*

With the approaching dawn, Elliot's hopes waned. He was all too aware of the dire consequences for a patient unable to nourish or hydrate themselves. He knew the risks of resorting to extreme medical measures to keep her alive. And he knew that their baby, born so prematurely, would likely not survive.

Tears streaming down his face, Elliot gently withdrew his hand from Ebba's and tried to collect himself. Even her touch caused him immense pain, a reminder of how fragile she had become. But then, in a sudden convulsion, Ebba's body jolted and her eyes snapped open as she gasped for air. Her weak lungs wheezed and bubbled with each breath, and she broke out in a cold sweat. Yet despite it all, her eyes found Elliot's and she managed a feeble smile.

It hit him like a tidal wave—hope flooding his heart—as he watched her struggle to regain consciousness. Soon enough, her gaze remained fixed on him. That small gesture filled Elliot with more joy and relief than he ever thought possible.

With a deep breath, he leaned in closer to her, his hand reaching out to tenderly stroke her pale cheek.

"Ebba," he whispered hoarsely. "Can you hear me?"

Her eyelids fluttered open and she turned towards him, her hazy eyes still clouded with pain and exhaustion. But there was a glimmer of recognition in them, and that was all that mattered in that moment.

"I can hear you," she murmured weakly, attempting to reach for his hand but failing.

"I'm sorry—I didn't mean to worry you."

Tears pricked at Elliot's eyes as he shook his head, his thumb continuing to caress her cheek gently.

"Don't apologise," he said fiercely. "You're alive—you're here with me."

He grasped her hand tightly in his own, pouring every ounce of love and strength he had into her fragile body.

"You are going to fight this," he declared firmly. "You are going to survive and we will have our future together—you, me, and our little one."

CHAPTER 38

True to her word, Ebba was soon back on her feet after some expert care from Elliot, Gwen and Sian, and a generous sprinkling of luck.

Elliot told her to rest, but she defied him again, of course. So, he asked Gwen and Sian to keep an eye on her in case she overdid it again.

Gwen did regular checks and was always impressed with the baby's growth, which seemed unaffected by her illness. But that changed at the last check.

"Ebba," she said as she listened with the newfangled fetoscope, "If I am not mistaken, you are going to have twins!"

The young doctor gasped at the news. She had worried about raising one child on top of their mammoth workload, but now there were going to be two souls to welcome.

"Don't worry, lass. We'll pitch in and help. Sian's coped with little Gethin. There will be plenty of love and affection to go around for these two."

"Good, because I am going to need it," said Ebba as she heaved herself off the examination bed to tell Elliot the news.

She wondered how he would take the news that he was going to be a father of two on his first accidental attempt at parenthood.

Gwen, ever the attentive midwife, kept a close eye on Ebba throughout her pregnancy. Ebba managed to keep working until almost reaching her estimated due date, by which time she was enormous. When the date was less than a fortnight away, she found herself growing increasingly anxious about the prospect of delivering twins.

Despite her medical expertise and the support of her skilled colleagues, the thought of giving birth to twins weighed heavily on her mind. That worry worsened when Gwen suspected some complications had arisen. One of the babies seemed to be breech, its tiny body stubbornly resisting the natural order of birth. No amount of manipulation would get the little one to comply.

> "Ebba, my dear," Gwen said gently, "it seems one of your little ones is determined to make a grand entrance. We'll need to be extra careful and patient. Nothing to worry about. I will be with you."

But the news did worry Ebba. She knew the risks were immense: a tangled umbilical cord cutting off precious nutrients to the baby, the possibility of the baby's head becoming lodged, or even worse, potential injuries for both mother and child during delivery.

As labour began, Gwen conducted a thorough assessment by palpating Ebba's abdomen to determine the position of the babies. Elliot chose to wait outside since Gwen and Sian had much more experience with childbirth.

> "This one definitely takes after you, Ebba. You can't be made to do something either," Gwen joked, hoping her nerves didn't show.

Despite the levity, Ebba could see Gwen's face was grim as she worked so hard to turn the infant, but failed.

> "Come on, little one," she murmured, her voice strained with concentration. "Ease yourself along just an inch or two."

> "Ebba, I'm going to ask you to move. I want you to kneel for me. Can you do that? We're going to use the weight of the baby's body to help you deliver the babies."

Ebba nodded, her jaw clenched as another contraction rippled through her body. Gwen positioned her carefully, helping to shift her hips as she took a kneeling position.

As the labour progressed, with great difficulty, Gwen maintained a hands-off approach, allowing the baby's rear and legs to emerge naturally. She knew that premature intervention could lead to complications, so she focused on providing reassurance and support to Ebba.

> "You're doing wonderfully," Gwen murmured, her voice calm and steady. "Trust your body and trust your baby."

Sian, ever the diligent assistant, wiped Ebba's brow with a cool cloth and offered words of encouragement and comfort.

> "You're so strong, Ebba. Just a little longer, and you'll be holding your beautiful twins."

As the first baby's body emerged up to the shoulders, Gwen gently manipulated each tiny arm out to ensure they didn't become trapped. Her skilled hands worked deftly yet gently.

The most critical moment arrived as the first baby's head began to emerge. Gwen's focus intensified; her years of experience guiding her every move. She closely monitored the baby's progress.

> "Almost there, Ebba," Gwen encouraged, her hands supporting the baby's delicate head. "One more push, and your first little one will be here."

With a final, determined effort, Ebba brought her first twin into the world. Gwen quickly cleared the baby's airway, stimulating a lusty cry that filled the room with joy and relief. As Sian cleaned the newborn, Gwen prepared for the arrival of the second baby, who proved to be far less demanding. Soon both babies were nestled in Ebba's arms, their tiny faces scrunched up against the bright light of the world.

> "You'd better come in, Elliot. She's done it!" Gwen said, her voice thick with emotion. "You have two lovely, healthy babies. Both boys. I'm so proud of you."

Ebba looked up at them all, tears of gratitude and exhaustion streaming down her face.

> "I couldn't have done it without you, especially you, Gwen. Thank you for everything."

Gwen squeezed Ebba's hand; a smile spread across her face.

> "That's what I'm here for, my dear. Always."

As the room settled into a contented silence, broken only by the soft coos and gurgles of the newborns, Gwen marvelled at the strength and resilience of the woman before her. Ebba had faced so many challenges; so many trials in her life yet she had emerged victorious once again—her spirit unbroken and her heart full of love.

It was moments like these that made Gwen reflect on her profession. It was profoundly rewarding to be a part of such a transformative experience—to guide and support women through the most vulnerable and powerful moments of their lives. It was a calling; a true labour of love.

"Do they have names yet, Elliot?" Sian asked.

"Archie and George," Elliot whispered, his voice filled with awe as he stroked the heads of his beautiful newborn sons. "They are perfect—both of them. Absolutely perfect."

CHAPTER 39

The entire village celebrated the Chadwick births. Little Billy ran to the church, and Reverend Jenkins soon had the bells ringing, their peals carrying the joyous news across the valley. Well-wishers streamed to the clinic, their arms laden with simple gifts and bright smiles on their faces.

Gwen sent one visitor up to see the new mother, Elizabeth Huntington, her usual crisp and impeccable appearance softened by the warmth in her eyes as she slipped into Ebba's room.

> "You don't know me very well, but I know a lot about you. I have been fighting for your cause ever since you arrived."
>
> "You have?"
>
> "Yes—it was me," Elizabeth whispered. "I was the mystery benefactor behind the donations to the clinic. Only Gwen knew."

Ebba looked furious at this news. Her eyes widened as a rush of conflicting emotions washed over her. Gratitude warred with confusion, and a flicker of anger sparked in her heart.

> "Gwen knew?"

"Please don't be angry. She deduced my identity and I made her swear to secrecy. If Charles found out I was aiding the men, especially during the strike—well, you can imagine his response! But I couldn't let you fight this battle alone. Henry Blackwood and I always felt that the men deserved more recognition and reward for their bravery and loyalty. She only kept it a secret to strengthen your campaign and the very good work you do here."

Ebba closed her eyes, taking a moment to process this revelation. When she opened them again, her thinking was as clear as her vision.

"Thank you," she whispered, squeezing Elizabeth's hand. "For everything. And your secret is still safe with me."

*

In the weeks that followed, flu cases decreased and more investment flowed into the healthcare scheme at Cwmgryf. An architect arrived to draw up plans to transform the outbuilding clinic into a proper cottage hospital, partly thanks to the last of Elizabeth's inheritance.

Within two months, the once cramped and makeshift rooms were now bright and airy, filled with the latest medical equipment. Plans were made to recruit a team of nurses. It was the flagship facility offering essential care and avoiding the risky journey to Cardiff.

As Ebba adjusted to motherhood, she watched her dream hospital take shape brick by brick. She loved nothing more than showing visitors around while Elliot talked about the specifics from his research. The thought of helping not only Cwmgryf but also neighbouring valleys in the parish, made her incredibly proud. She could barely imagine how proud she would be if all local government boards followed suit.

CHAPTER 40

It was a typical afternoon at the new medical centre, still resembling a construction site. Sadly, injuries were all too common.

> "That's quite a deep gash you've got there, Billy. Remember to wear your thickest leather gloves on your shifts," scolded Ebba. "unless you want to lose a finger next time?"
>
> "Sorry, Ebba."
>
> "Alright, let's clean it up again, shall we?"

As she tended to Billy's hand, the door to the clinic swung open, startling Ebba. Elliot poked his head out from behind a stack of papers.

Sian burst into the room, her face flushed and her usually immaculate bun unravelling from her hasty pace. She waved a newspaper excitedly as if it were a prized possession just won at the fair.

> "Dr Ebba! Dr Elliot! Have you seen the news?"

Sian yelled as she rushed towards them, nearly tripping over herself.

> "Be careful, Sian! I doubt you run around like that at Mrs Morgan's shop," cautioned Ebba. "What's on earth is going on? Is everything in order?" asked Ebba with an undertone of worry.

Having lived in a mining village for so long, unexpected news was rarely good, but Sian's eyes sparkled with joy and anticipation. She handed Ebba the newspaper and pointed at the headline.

> "Look! The government has formed a select committee headed by William Mabon. They're launching a fundraising campaign to trial two more healthcare schemes in Carmarthenshire and Monmouthshire!"

After patching up Billy, Elliot crossed the room in a few long strides to read the article over Ebba's shoulder. His eyes widened in awe.

> "By Jove, this is monumental news."

Sian nodded eagerly, barely containing her enthusiasm.

> "Can't you see what this means for us? For Cwmgryf? The Salvation Army, The Trust, and of course, you and Elliot. All your hard work, the challenges you've faced to provide quality medical care for the workers and their families—it could become the standard everywhere. I'm shaking with excitement, and I'm just a volunteer. You two have devoted years of your lives to reach this moment!"

Ebba felt a lump form in her throat. To think that their small clinic, born out of one of John and Jess Chadwick's ideas, could have such a significant impact—it was almost too much to comprehend.

"This is amazing news, Sian. Truly incredible."

Ebba glanced at Elliot, noticing the proud set of his jaw and the determined gleam in his eye.

They had fought tirelessly for this moment. Countless late nights tending to the sick and injured, battling scepticism from all sides, stretching meagre resources as far as they could go, and fundraising even when they had little to spare. And now, there was a chance that their work would be recognised and validated on a regional, maybe even national scale—it filled Ebba with an even greater sense of fierce hope than she was born with.

Elliot pulled Ebba aside.

> "We couldn't have done this without the support of our community," he said solemnly. "The trust they've placed in us, even after what happened with your father and Bryn Jones stirring up trouble—the faith they've shown—well, it's humbling."
>
> "I think we should celebrate at the May Day Miner's March! Who's with me?" shouted Sian.

The resounding cheer that followed nearly shook the roof off the new building.

*

The Miners' May Day March was a kaleidoscope of colours and sounds, just like the fete when the Chadwicks arrived. Bunting and banners in bold hues of red, green, and blue fluttered in the gentle breeze. The air sparkled with the lively melodies of traditional folk songs, like 'The Little Saucepan', 'Sosban fach,' intertwined with the excited chatter and laughter of the gathered crowd.

Ebba and Elliot stood side by side on the bandstand, their hearts swelling with a profound sense of gratitude and belonging. As they looked out at the sea of faces before them, emotions caught in their throats. These were the people they had fought for, families they had tended to in sickness and health, a community that had welcomed them with open arms and trusting hearts, and a community that proved a more caring society where the working classes were lifted up instead of trampled down.

Elliot stepped forward, his voice ringing out clear and strong across the green.

> "People of Cwmgryf, we stand before you today with hearts full of appreciation and admiration. When Ebba and I first arrived in this village, we were strangers, outsiders with a dream of making a difference. But you embraced us, trusted us, even when some naysayers publicly questioned us and our motives. You allowed us to become a part of your lives. From trying to work out solutions to protracted colliery problems, to protest marches to Cardiff, to working hard to make the new seam profitable, you have supported us at every turn. On behalf of my wife

and our baby sons, Archie and George—thank you from the bottom of our hearts."

Ebba joined him, her own voice loud and powerful.

"Ladies and gentlemen, we have witnessed your strength, resilience, and unwavering determination to build a better future for yourselves and your children. You have faced adversity with courage and compassion, showing us the true meaning of community. Please join us at the new cottage hospital—"

There was another roar of applause and cheering voices.

"—where a mystery benefactor has provided us with a lovely spread of local food and drinks."

The cheering reached an ear-splitting volume as they left the bandstand. Ebba's gaze drifted over the crowd. Just to the left side, Gwen and Llewellyn were holding Archie and George.

Next to them were Sian and Rhys, their eyes shining with joy and love. They were in their own world as Rhys tickled young Gethin, the boy reaching for his face and hands, craving his touch.

Beyond them, she saw countless others: miners and their families, shopkeepers, teachers, Reverend Jenkins, labourers, cart boys, railway men, laundresses, seamstresses—all united in their shared hopes and dreams.

Amidst the joyous celebrations, Sian and Rhys fought their way towards Ebba and Elliot. Sian's voice rang out clear and jubilant.

"We have some wonderful news to share with you!"

Rhys exchanged a loving glance with Sian before announcing:

"I've asked Sian to marry me, and she said yes!"

Ebba gasped, her hands flying to her mouth in delighted surprise.

"Oh, Sian! That's absolutely wonderful! Congratulations!"

She embraced her friend, feeling the joy radiating from Sian's every pore.

Elliot clapped Rhys on the back, his grin stretching from ear to ear.

"Well done, Mr Davies! You've found yourself a real treasure in Sian. I couldn't be happier for you both."

"Of course, Rhys and I will wait a bit longer out of respect for my late Gethin, but he would be happy to see us together now. We were close friends before, and our love has only grown stronger through the challenges we've faced. And baby

Gethin adores Rhys, which is an added blessing that came from all the chaos we went through."

"I suppose that means you're staying in Cwmgryf then?" Ebba added coyly.

"Most definitely, doctor," Rhys said with a smile.

"Well, there must be something in the air today," added Gwen, overhearing the happy announcement, her eyes sparkling in the sunlight.

Llewellyn took Gwen's hand discretely.

"We've set a date for our wedding! We've been engaged for so long, waiting to see what happened to the village and the colliery, and now, well, we think it's the right time to get hitched."

Sian clapped her hands together, her face alight with happiness.

"That's fantastic, Gwen! We'll be there to celebrate with you, come hell or high water!"

"Be there? I was thinking of a joint wedding! It's not like we have parents who can pay for everything! The two shillings of saving we have between us won't go far!" Gwen chuckled.

As the friends embraced, their laughter mingling with the music and the chatter of the crowd, Ebba felt a warm glow spreading through her chest. In the midst of all the struggles and uncertainties, these moments of pure, unadulterated joy were a reminder of what truly mattered: love, friendship, and the unbreakable bonds that held their community and the fabric of their lives together.

CHAPTER 41

As the May Day March festivities continued, Ebba and Elliot found themselves surrounded by the grateful faces of the villagers they had come to know and love. Old Mary Evans, her weathered hands clasped around Ebba's, her eyes brimming with tears, spoke softly:

> "Dr Chadwick, I don't know what we would've done without you. My son's hand is perfect now. You've brought hope back to Cwmgryf. And I am sure you had something to do with in getting rid of that beast Gerald Price."

Ebba, deeply touched by the woman's words, squeezed her hands gently.

> "It's been an honour to serve this community, Mrs Evans. We're all in this together, and together, we'll build a brighter future for Cwmgryf."

> "Oi! Doctor Elliot! Just wanted to say thanks," said Tom Watts. "You've given us men a voice, and that means more than you can ever know!"

> "It's been a privilege," Elliot said as he clasped the man's shoulder.

As the day wore on, the sense of unity and camaraderie only grew stronger. Long tables set up, groaning under the weight of homemade dishes and delicacies were soon emptied. Laughter and conversation flowed freely as the villagers shared stories and dreams, their faces alight with joy and hope.

Music filled the air, with the villagers dancing, their feet tapping to the lively rhythms of fiddles, accordions, brass bands and singers. Ebba and Elliot found themselves swept up in the merriment, twirling and laughing alongside their friends and neighbours, clutching their precious boys close to them, their cherubic faces beaming for hours.

In that moment, the struggles and hardships of the past seemed to melt away, replaced by a profound sense of belonging and purpose.

As the sun set and the festivities began to wind down the community started to disperse. They walked arm in arm, their faces etched with a renewed sense of purpose and determination. The laughter and chatter gradually faded, replaced by a contemplative silence as they made their way back to their homes, each lost in their own thoughts.

As Ebba gazed out over the now empty green, Ebba couldn't help but reflect on the incredible journey that had brought them to this point. The challenges they had faced, the obstacles they had overcome, and the unbreakable bonds they had forged along the way. It seemed like a lifetime ago that she and Elliot had first set foot in this village, their hearts full of hope and their minds brimming with dreams of making a difference.

Later that night, as they rocked their boys to sleep in their matching moses baskets, Elliot, sensing his wife's emotions, drew her close, his voice soft and tender.

"If a fortune teller told me where our lives would lead when I found you on that bitterly cold night in London, barely alive, I would never have believed them. And although we have had our fair share of hardships, I have everything I could ever ask for. I love you, Doctor Chadwick! And these two of course," he said leaning over to see his sons dozing peacefully, worn out by all the excitement of the day, much like their parents.

EPILOGUE

Some months later.

Ebba stood before the mirror in her bedroom, smoothing down the lilac dress she and Gwen had carefully handcrafted. She smiled as her fingers traced the delicate lace at the wrists.

Elliot entered the room, looking dashing in his jet black frock coat and crisp white shirt.

> "A double wedding," Ebba mused. "Trust Gwen and Sian to do things their own way."
>
> "Well, they've had a good teacher," Elliot joked, winking at his beloved, fiery wife. "Are my little sailors ready?"

Archie and George, now precocious toddlers, wobbled over to their father with beaming faces. They were dressed in adorable navy suits, a gift from Llewelyn, ready for their role as pages in the ceremony.

Ebba's gaze drifted to the photo on her bedside table: a snapshot of the May Day March. Gwen and Sian stood arm in arm, their fiancés proudly behind them, their faces filled with hope for the future.

As they entered St David's Chapel, Ebba marvelled at the vibrant garlands draping the pews and the elegant bows adorning the altar—a perfect blend of Gwen and Sian's tastes.

Reverend Jenkins stood at the front with kind eyes that crinkled at the corners as he greeted guests. Even Uncle Ifan had made the journey, looking fit and hearty as he chatted with Mary Evans.

The ceremony was a beautiful testament to love and hope. As the two couples exchanged vows beneath the kaleidoscope of colours cast by the sunlit stained-glass windows, there wasn't a single dry eye in the church. When they shared their first kisses as newlyweds outside of church, guests erupted in cheers, tossing small handfuls of wheat to celebrate their union.

The reception at the Working Men's Club was a joyous affair; even the once dreary interior was transformed with fresh flowers and foliage, as well as cheerful handmade paper chains made at the Sunday School.

Soon, laughter and music filled the air as the newlyweds danced a lively jig, inviting guests to join in the merriment.

As the celebration wound down, Ebba and Elliot bid their farewells, holding on to Archie and George.

> "By the way, Elliot, did Sian ever tell you what Cwmgryf means in Welsh?"
>
> "No," he said, raising an eyebrow.

"It means: 'The Valley of the Strong.' I rather like that, don't you?"

"It's perfect," he said, before giving her the gentlest of kisses.

Dive into 'Widow of the Valley' and immerse yourself in another stirring transformation of a broken and betrayed Welsh widow into a resilient woman, in a tale that masterfully combines saga, heartfelt emotion, and vivid historical detail.

Enjoy a free book, 'The Pit Lad's Mother' when you sign up to my newsletter.

THE PIT LAD'S MOTHER

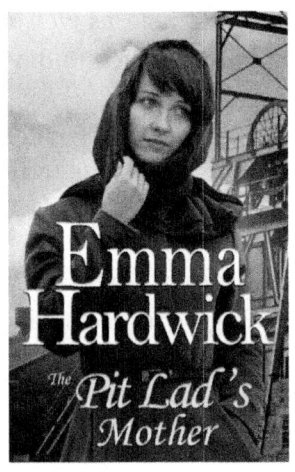

Get your FREE copy now.

Mary Bartram dreads disaster striking again. Will her boy be next?

1840s Northumberland

When fire rips through Bingham's Colliery, the Bartram family lose a beloved husband, father, and breadwinner.

Now that Mary Bartram is in dire financial straits, she has no choice but to send youngest son to work the trap doors in the treacherous mine.

What will happen to poor, unfortunate Mary if the reaper visits again? And what of the lad, working alone in the pitch black. How does loyal little Peter cope when every unexplained noise makes him ever more concerned? Is his mind playing tricks? Is his older brother teasing him? Could it be his late father trying to reassure the boy?

Is the family destined for the workhouse without money in the coffers? Can Lady Luck finally bring the widow the peace she so desperately needs?

[Click here to get your free book and find out now](https://dl.bookfunnel.com/rzk3cxqdks).

(https://dl.bookfunnel.com/rzk3cxqdks)

THE WIDOW OF THE VALLEY

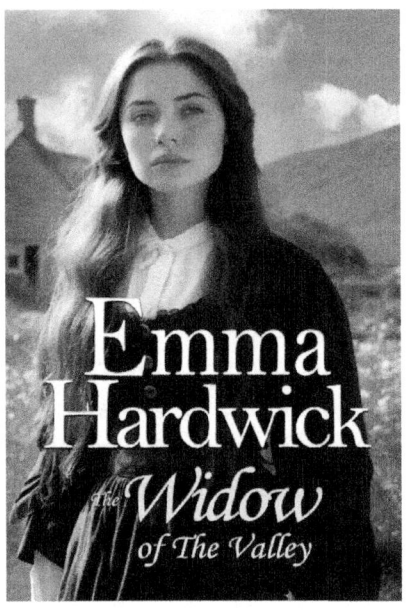

Check out 'Widow of the Valley' on Amazon.

Courage amidst grief: A young Welsh widow's fight for hope and a brighter future.

1880s Glamorgan

From the humble backstreets of Cardiff to the lush valleys of South Wales, new bride Derryn dreams of a brighter, love-filled life. However, when a devastating colliery disaster strikes, it shatters her world, leaving her a grieving widow wrestling with aching solitude.

Soon, cruel rumours of her late husband's infidelity circulate the remote mining village, intensifying her heartache. Shunned by the unsympathetic mine owner and the scornful eyes of the villagers, Derryn finds solace in the company of another local outcast and the numbing embrace of the bottle.

As her resources deplete, the prospect of destitution looms. Will Derryn succumb to the despair of poverty and loneliness, or can the same merciless fate that shattered her dreams help her mend the broken pieces?

Immerse yourself in this gripping historical family saga today. Experience the trials and triumphs of Derryn, a strong woman who grapples with societal rejection, personal betrayal, and profound grief, as she bravely navigates towards a second chance at love and life.

Check out 'Widow of the Valley' on Amazon.

ABOUT THE AUTHOR

Thanks so much for your support. I really appreciate it. Being able to write my books is a dream come true and I never take a second of this opportunity for granted. If you want to find out some more about me, you can browse my website.

www.emmahardwick.co.uk

You can also connect with me on Facebook at :

www.facebook.com/emmahardwickauthor

If the mood takes you, you can send me an email at:

hello@emmahardwick.co.uk

Printed in Great Britain
by Amazon